MODERN CLASSICS
MAGIC

Publisher / Co-CEO: Jon Goldwater
Co-President / Editor-In-Chief: Victor Gorelick
Co-President: Mike Pellerito
Chief Creative Officer: Roberto Aguirre-Sacasa
Chief Operating Officer: William Mooar
Chief Financial Officer: Robert Wintle
Director: Jonathan Betancourt
Senior Director of Editorial: Jamie Lee Rotante
Art Director: Vincent Lovallo
Director of Publicity & Social Media: Ron Cacace
Production Manager: Stephen Oswald
Lead Designer: Kari McLachlan
Associate Editor: Carlos Antunes
Co-CEO: Nancy Silberkleit

Published by Archie Comic Publications, Inc. 629 Fifth Avenue, Pelham, NY 10803-1242

ISBN: 978-1-64576-907-1

STORIES

DAN PARENT, RON ROBBINS,
BILL BETTWY, BILL GOLLIHER, FRANCIS BONNET,
JAMIE L. ROTANTE, JACK MORELLI, TANIA DEL RIO,
ANGELO DECESARE & CRAIG BOLDMAN

ART

DAN PARENT, PAT KENNEDY, TIM KENNEDY,
JEFF SHULTZ, BILL GALVAN, BILL GOLLIHER, BOB SMITH,
JIM AMASH, BEN GALVAN, GLENN WHITMORE,
JACK MORELLI & ROSARIO "TITO" PEÑA

CONTENTS

2021 has come and gone and to say it was a special year for Archie is an understatement! It was, in fact, a very momentous year as we celebrated Archie's landmark 80th anniversary! And that celebration permeated throughout many of our modern classic stories over the course of the year—including launching a special digest series, *Archie's 80th Anniversary Digest*, each of the five issues featuring a brand-new story that saw Archie exploring his past in fun ways!

There was another character who also shared the spotlight with Archie (and will continue to throughout 2022, as we celebrate her 60th anniversary to come)—and that's everyone's favorite teenage witch, Sabrina Spellman. Before she found herself in a special cameo role on the CW TV series *Riverdale*, Sabrina bedazzled us, with not only the return of the *Chilling Adventure of Sabrina* comic, but also a number of appearances in digest stories.

This new year will continue a celebration of all things Archie and his friends, but for now, turn the page to be spellbound by some of the most memorable recent classic-style Archie stories!

ARCHIE COMICS

Archie in ICE, ICE BABY!

NOTHING LIKE SKATING ON OLD LAKE DOYLE, ARCHIE!

EXCEPT THAT IT'S SO UNBEARABLY COLD, BETTY!

DAN PARENT STORY & PENCILS

BOB SMITH INKS

GLENN WHITMORE COLORS

JACK MORELLI LETTERS

$

SO...
WHAT'S THIS?!
WELCOME TO "CHOCO-LICIOUS"!
A & J
Choco-Licious

WE'RE SELLING JUG'S HOT CHOCOLATE, VERONICA!
HE'S THE TALENT... I'M THE BRAINS BEHIND THE BUSINESS!

SOUNDS LIKE A RECIPE FOR DISASTER!
NO COCOA FOR YOU!

SOON...
JUGHEAD! WE'RE SOLD OUT! WE'RE A HIT!
I'LL HAVE TO MAKE A DOUBLE-BATCH TOMORROW!
2

THE NEXT DAY...
IT'S SNOWING LIKE CRAZY! PERFECT HOT CHOCOLATE WEATHER!
Choco-Licious
GUYS! YOU'D BETTER PACK UP! THERE'S A BLIZZARD ON THE WAY!!
OCO-Licious
A BLIZZARD! YOU KNOW WHAT THAT MEANS!
A BLIZZARD OF CASH!
I'M GOING HOME BEFORE IT HITS!
Choco-Licious
ME TOO!
THAT'S OKAY! MORE CHOCOLATEY GOODNESS FOR US!
IT IS GETTING PRETTY--
FWAP
--WINDY!
3

-Licious
OKAY! MAYBE WE'D BETTER CLOSE UP SHOP FOR TODAY!
YEAH, LET'S...
A & J
WHOOOO
WE'RE TAKING OFF ACROSS THE LAKE!
HELP!
HOW DO WE STOP THIS CRAZY THING?!
I THINK THAT'S UP TO MOTHER NATURE!
ZOOM
A & J
WELL, WE'RE OFF THE LAKE...
AND SLIDING INTO TOWN!
4

ZOOM
A & J
ARCHIE?! JUGHEAD?!
HI, POP!
BYE, POP!
?!
WE'RE HEADED FOR THAT BIG SNOWPILE!
PWOMP
SSSS
SSSS
ON THE BRIGHT SIDE, THESE HOT CONTAINERS HAVE MELTED US TO FREEDOM!
ONE HOT COCOA TO GO, PLEASE!
END

in
POP's
PURR-FECT BIRTHDAY

RON ROBBINS WRITER
The FAB K-BROS! PENCILS
BOB SMITH INKS
GLENN WHITMORE COLORS
JACK MORELLI LETTERS
THANKS FOR THE SURPRISE BIRTHDAY DINNER, KIDS! WHERE ARE WE HEADED?
POP's
YOU'LL SEE!
The Spruce
HERE WE ARE!
POP, THIS IS A BRAND NEW RESTAURANT BY CELEBRITY RESTAURATEUR PRESTON PALMER! DADDY'S AN INVESTOR!

WELCOME TO THE SPRUCE... POP TATE!?
HELLO, PALMER.

YOU TWO KNOW EACH OTHER?
INDEED.
WELL, COME ON INSIDE! LET'S GET YOU ALL SEATED.
1

THIS PLACE IS AWESOME!
THANKS, ARCHIE! BUILDING SUCCESSFUL RESTAURANTS LIKE The SPRUCE IS MY PASSION. I JUST THROW MYSELF INTO IT.
TOO BAD BOTTOMLESS PITS AREN'T HIS PASSION.

WHAT WAS THAT, POP? I COULDN'T HEAR YOU OVER THE SWEET SOUND OF SUCCESS.
I'M PRETTY SURE THAT'S JUST A STRAY CAT.

Oh, COME ON NOW, POP. YOU REALLY SHOULDN'T BE SO JEALOUS.
NO, I MEAN I'M PRETTY SURE I JUST SAW TWO MORE CATS RUN OUT OF THE KITCHEN!

NO! NOT TODAY! I HAVE A MAJOR FOOD CRITIC AT TABLE NINE!
GEE, POP-- WHAT GIVES?
I'M SORRY, KIDS. PALMER AND I GO WAY BACK. WE GREW UP TOGETHER AND ALWAYS HAD A VERY CONTENTIOUS RELATIONSHIP. MUCH LIKE YOU TWO BOYS!
2

BOOF
SPLAT
KRASH
KLANG
HOMK
The Spruce
BLATT

EVERYTHING SEEMS TO BE GOING WRONG! HOW TERRIBLE!
IS IT?
COME ON, POP. REG AND I DON'T ALWAYS GET ALONG, BUT WE'D NEVER LET EACH OTHER SUFFER!

YOU GOT THAT RIGHT, BUDDY.

YOU'RE RIGHT, KIDS. LET'S GET TO WORK!

CLAP
COME ON, V! LET'S DO THIS!
4

YOU ALL TRULY SAVED THE NIGHT! I'M ETERNALLY GRATEFUL!
THE PLEASURE WAS OURS, PALMER! NOTHING COULD MAKE THIS BIRTHDAY ANY BETTER!

HOW ABOUT A BRAND NEW CAT!?
The END

Archie in I'm DIGGIN' IT!

OKAY, MOM! ALL FINISHED!
WOW! YOU CERTAINLY LOOK FINISHED!

DAN PARENT STORY
JEFF SHULTZ: PENCILS
JIM AMASH INKS
GLENN WHITMORE COLORS
JACK MORELLI LETTERS

YEAH, THAT WAS ONE MESSY JOB!
BUT IT SURE WILL LOOK NICE WHEN THOSE TULIPS POP UP!
SCRUB SCRUB
SHOOSH
H-Huh?!
WHO'S THAT IN OUR GARDEN?!
IT LOOKS LIKE A GROUNDHOG!
AND HE'S EATING MY HANDIWORK!
GET OUT OF OUR GARDEN!
ARCHIE?!
FIND A BUFFET SOMEWHERE ELSE, YOU TULIP THIEF!
PUT THOSE BULBS--
--DOOOWN!
SLIP
2

HEE HEE!

ARCHIE!! GET INSIDE BEFORE THE NEIGHBORS TALK!
TOO LATE!

LATER...
THERE! MORE BULBS PLANTED!
AND WITH A FENCE THIS TIME!

GAK!
HE'S BACK!!
WHAT?!
Pbbbt!

HE DUG UNDER THE FENCE!
WHY DIDN'T YOU STOP HIM, MR. REYNOLDS?!

I WAS BUSY RECORDING HIM!
THIS WILL BE GREAT ON FLIP-FLOP!
3

LATER, AT POP'S...
ARCHIE! YOU'RE A STAR!
OR RATHER, A CO-STAR!

"GEORGIE" THE GROUNDHOG IS THE REAL STAR!
WHAT?!

FLOP
HEE-HEE!

HE GOT ALL THAT ON VIDEO?
AND THEN HE GOT HIM SNEAKING UNDER THAT JOKE OF A FENCE YOU PUT UP!
POP'S

EVERYONE LOVES GEORGIE! HE'S GOT 30,000 LIKES!
THAT LITTLE BUCK-TOOTHED BULB BANDIT IS RUINING OUR GARDEN!

AND NOBODY CARES!!
POOR ARCHIE!
I'VE GOT AN IDEA!
4

THE NEXT DAY...
VERONICA! WHAT'S UP?
HI, ARCHIEKINS! MEET OUR GROUNDSKEEPER, ELLA!

WE HAVE A PRESENT FOR YOU!
THIS IS "GEORGINA"!

I FIGURE SHE'LL BE A GOOD DISTRACTION FOR GEORGIE!
LET'S HOPE!

LOOK! THEY'VE HIT IT OFF!
GOOD! RUN OFF TOGETHER! HAVE A NICE LIFE!

GREAT IDEA, RONNIE!
LOVE CONQUERS ALL!
LATER...

AWWW... LOOK AT THEM IN LOVE!
AND LOOK AT WHAT THEY'RE EATING-- MY MOM'S ROSES!
THE END

Archie in Teach Thanks!

ARCHIE, I THINK SHE HELPED YOU IN ENGLISH TO SAVE THE LANGUAGE! WHO PUTS EMOJIS IN A TERM PAPER?
HER TUTORING REALLY SAVED THE DAY FOR ME!
YOU SHOULD DO SOMETHING NICE FOR HER!
HEY, WE SHOULD DO SOMETHING NICE FOR ALL OUR TEACHERS!
LEAVING THEM ALONE ALL SUMMER IS PROBABLY THE BEST PRESENT WE CAN GIVE THEM!
HEY, ARCHIE -- I HAVE A GREAT IDEA! REMEMBER THAT PHOTOBOOK YOU GAVE YOUR PARENTS FOR THEIR ANNIVERSARY?
YOU MEAN THE ONE I ORDERED USING THE PHOTOS ON MY PHONE?
YES!
MY PARENTS REALLY LOVED THAT!
AND ALL I HAD TO DO WAS UPLOAD SOME PHOTOS TO THE PICTURE PLACE!
2

I'LL JUST USE SOME OF THE CANDID SCHOOL SHOTS I HAVE!

THEN WE CAN MAKE PHOTOBOOKS FOR ALL THE TEACHERS!
WHAT A GREAT IDEA!

A FEW DAYS LATER...
NOW I JUST HAVE TO UPLOAD MY "SCHOOL SHOTS" FOLDER...
...AND VOILA!
BEEP

I'LL TEXT THE GANG!
THESE PHOTOBOOKS SHOULD ARRIVE JUST IN TIME FOR THE END OF THE SCHOOL YEAR!

SO... ON THE VERY ABSOLUTE LAST DAY OF THE SCHOOL YEAR...
VERONICA, HAVE YOU HEARD FROM ARCHIE?
NO! WHERE ARE OUR PHOTO-BOOKS?!
3

HERE I AM! AND HERE THEY ARE!
I'M GOING TO GET THESE THANK YOU PICTURE BOOKS TO THE TEACHERS' LOUNGE!

ONE FOR EACH TEACHER AND YOU, MS. PHLIPS!
THANK YOU, ARCHIE! I'LL TELL THEM!

AND A FEW FOR US TO ENJOY!
UH... ARCHIE -- DID YOU SEE THIS YET?

WHAT IS THIS SUPPOSED TO BE ON THE COVER?
IT'S SUPPOSED TO BE A GROUP SHOT OF US!

BUT IT LOOKS LIKE MY ELBOW!
THIS WAS AFTER I GOT BITTEN BY THAT SPIDER LAST SUMMER!
I SNAPPED A PICTURE TO SHOW MY DOCTOR!

WHAT IS THIS?!
HA!
ARCHIE! THAT'S A PICTURE OF YOU FLEXING!
ACK!
4

AND A PICTURE OF ME WHEN I TORE MY PANTS!
HA! THAT WAS FUNNY!
OHMIGOSH! I UPLOADED THE WRONG FOLDER!
THESE PHOTOS WERE IN A FOLDER I WAS GOING TO DELETE!!
HOW HUMILIATING!
YOU TOOK A LOT OF RIDICULOUS PICTURES, ARCH!
HA!
HAHA HAHA!
THEY SEEM AMUSED!
OH, ARCHIE! THIS ALBUM OF COMICAL PHOTOS IS HILARIOUS!
HA HA!
WE APPRECIATE YOU THINKING OUTSIDE THE BOX! WAY OUTSIDE!
HA!
HA! HA!
THIS BORDERS ON SURREAL! YOU'RE A LAUGH RIOT, ARCHIE!
JUST CALL ME LAUGH WITH ARCHIE!
HA!
HA HA!
END

GET OUT OF HERE! ARCHIE'S FOUND A SIDE HUSTLE THAT HE'S *GOOD AT*?!

Archie IN MOW MANTLE, MOW PROBLEMS!

BILL BETTWY STORY

BILL GALVAN PENCILS

JIM AMASH INKS

GLENN WHITMORE COLORS

JACK MORELLI LETTERS

ARCHIE'S AWESOME LAWN SERVICE

17 DAYS WITHOUT ACCIDENT

VROOOOW

1

THANK YOU, ARCHIE! SEE YOU NEXT WEEK!
YOU GOT IT, MRS. WILEY!

ARCHIE'S AWESOME LAWN SERVICE, Huh?! SO YOU THINK YOU'RE A BIG SHOT NOW?
AWWW? NO, I DON'T THINK THAT!

I ALSO DON'T THINK I'M FITTING ANY MORE MONEY INTO MY WALLET!

NEED A RIDE, BETTY?
SURE!

KOFF! KOFF!
IF ARCHIE HAS ALL THIS MONEY TO SPEND ON DATES NOW, WHO'S GOING TO DATE ME?!
ARCHIE'S AWESOME LAWN SERVICE
2

SOON!
LOOK AT THIS! MANTLE'S MAGNIFICENT MOWS!
WHAT? NOW REGGIE STARTED A LAWN CARE SERVICE?
MANTLE'S MAGNIFICENT MOWS

THAT'S RIGHT, BETTY AND VERONICA! I'M TAKING THIS TOWN OVER--ONE LAWN AT A TIME!
MANTLE'S MAGNIFICENT MOWS

HEY! WHAT THE HECK IS THIS?!

REGGIE MANTLE STARTED HIS OWN LAWN CARE SERVICE! LOOK! HE HAS FLYERS POSTED ALL OVER TOWN!
!
MANTLE'S MAGNIFICENT MOWS
HE PAID TO HAVE FLYERS PRINTED?!

GOTTA SPEND MONEY TO MAKE MONEY, CARROT-TOP!

GOTTA SPEND MONEY, Huh?! WELL, LET'S PUT THAT TO THE TEST!
VROOM

3

Oh, WOW! LOOK AT THAT!
POP
MANTL MAGNI MOW

ARCHIE MUST'VE SPENT A LOT OF HIS LAWN MONEY ON THAT AD!
ARCHIE'S AWESOME LAWN SERVICE

MAYBE... BUT I'M SURE HE DIDN'T SPEND AS MUCH AS REGGIE!
WHOA! NOW THAT WILL GET PEOPLE'S ATTENTION!
MANTLE'S MAGNIFICENT MOWS

OR REGGIE'S FACE WILL GET THEM TO LOSE THEIR APPETITES!
MUNCH
MUNCH MUNCH

BZZZZZZZZ
ARCHIE'S AWESOME LAWN SERVICE
LOOK! THAT PLANE IS PULLING AN ARCHIE AD!
WOW! THE WHOLE TOWN WILL SEE THAT!
4

THAT'S IF ANYBODY IS LOOKING UP FROM THEIR PHONES--BECAUSE THEY'RE READING REGGIE'S TEXT BLASTS!
BING BING BZZZ

ARCHIE AND REGGIE MUST BE SO BUSY!
AND MAKING LOTS OF MONEY!

THERE YOU BIG SHOTS ARE!
YOU TWO SHOULD SPEND SOME OF THAT GREEN YOU'RE MAKING ON TAKING US TO A FANCY RESTAURANT!

WE'D LOVE TO, GIRLS--BUT WE CAN'T!
WHY NOT?!
WE SPENT ALL OF OUR MONEY ON THOSE ADS! AND NOW WE'VE GOT SO MUCH WORK, WE HAVE NO TIME!
WE'LL BE MOWING UNTIL IT'S SNOWING!
END

Archie in RUFF Summer!

DAN PARENT STORY & PENCILS
BOB SMITH INKS
GLENN WHITMORE COLORS
JACK MORELLI LETTERS

LIFEGUARD DUTY CAN BE A BIT... BORING.

BUT IT'S A JOB...

WHAT'S UP, VEGAS?
DO YOU HEAR SOME-THING?
WHERE'S HE GOING?
SPLASH
I'VE GOT A CRAMP IN MY LEG!!
SPLASH
HEY! THANKS, BUDDY!
WILL YOU LOOK AT THAT!
I DIDN'T SEE HIM!
2

BUT VEGAS OBVIOUSLY COULD HEAR HIM!
GOTTA LOVE THAT DOGGIE HEAR-ING!

THE NEXT DAY...
GREAT JOB, VEGAS!
HOORAY, VEGAS!

SO...
VEGAS! DO YOU HEAR SOMETHING AGAIN?

EEK!
WHAT'S GOING ON?!
HE'S TRYING TO SAVE YOU!

BUT I DON'T NEED SAVING... WE'RE PLAYING!
OH, WELL!

HE MEANT WELL!
VEGAS, YOU NUT!
3

NOT EVERYBODY NEEDS SAVING, VEGAS!
BUT YOU ARE MY GOOD BOY!

THE NEXT DAY...
VEGAS! WHO DO YOU HAVE THERE?
SPLOOSH

MY NAME IS BECKY!
I JUST STEPPED INTO THE WATER AND HE PULLED ME OUT!

SORRY, BECKY! VEGAS HAS BEEN GETTING CARRIED AWAY!

NOW VEGAS--LEAVE THE LIFEGUARDING TO ME! AND IF YOU MUST SAVE SOMEONE...

...PLEASE MAKE SURE THEY WANT TO BE SAVED!
I THINK I CAN HELP!
4

THE NEXT DAY...
VEGAS, MEET Fifi!!

I FIGURE A DISTRACTION WILL DO VEGAS GOOD!
GOOD THINKING, VERONICA!

HELP! HELP!
DUTY CALLS!

LOOK AT VEGAS! HE'S NOT NOTICING ANYTHING BUT FIFI!

THERE! HE'S ALL TAKEN CARE OF!
I CAN'T BELIEVE VEGAS DIDN'T EVEN NOTICE!

LOOKS LIKE HE'S MORE FOCUSED ON GUARDING SOMEONE ELSE!!
END

Archie in NO TEEN IS AN ISLAND!
THANKS TO TONI AND EVERYONE FOR COMING ALONG ON MY INFLATABLE MEGA-ISLAND'S MAIDEN VOYAGE!
ARE YOU KIDDING, VERONICA?!
I'VE SEEN THESE THINGS IN STORES BEFORE, BUT THIS ONE IS KILLER!!
PFFFT
BILL GOLLIHER STORY
The KENNEDY BROTHERS PENCILS
JIM AMASH INKS
GLENN WHITMORE COLORS
JACK MORELLI LETTERS
ONCE WE GET OUT PAST THE BREAKERS, WE CAN ENJOY A DAY OF CAREFREE FUN AND SUN!
!
SOUNDS MARVEL-OUS!
WE EVEN HAVE THE DRINK COOLER AND SNACK BIN FULLY LOADED!
WHY DO YOU THINK I'M COMING ALONG?!
1

SOON...
THAT DOES IT! WE'RE AT SEA! THE INSTRUCTIONS SAY TO DROP THE INCLUDED ANCHOR TO STAY IN PLACE, ARCHIE!
AYE-AYE, CAP'N!
!
SPLOOSH
KLONK

NOW I OFFICIALLY DECLARE MY SHIP A PARTY ZONE!
YEAH! KEEP THE MUSIC BLASTING!

LATER
THIS IS THE LIFE, CHUCK! SOME-ONE SHOULD'VE THOUGHT OF THIS SOONER!
I DUNNO, NANCY... SOMETHING SEEMS A BIT WEIRD...

WHAT DO YOU MEAN?
WELL... I DON'T SEE THE BEACH ANYMORE! IT WAS THERE EARLIER!

HOW COULD THAT BE?! I HAD ARCHIE THROW OUT THE ANCHOR!
BUT NOTHING'S TIED ON TO THIS CLEAT!
WHAT?!!...
2

ARCHIE! YOU DIDN'T TIE THE ANCHOR LINE TO THE CLEAT! IT SAYS TO DO THAT RIGHT HERE!!
HOW WOULD I KNOW?! YOU HAD THE INSTRUCTIONS!
MANUAL
YOU JUST SAID 'DROP THE ANCHOR.'!
Oh, NO!! WE'VE BEEN ADRIFT ALL THIS TIME! THERE'S NO TELLING WHERE WE ARE!!
I'LL CALL FOR HELP! UH-OH! I DON'T HAVE A SIGNAL!
I DON'T THINK ANYONE DOES! WE'RE TOO FAR OUT!!
WE'RE AT NATURE'S MERCY!
AT LEAST WE HAVE PLENTY TO DRINK AND EAT... HEY! IT'S EMPTY!!
BURP!
SORRY, I GUESS I GOT CARRIED AWAY!
SHOULD SOMEONE GO FOR ASSISTANCE?
THAT DOESN'T SOUND SAFE!
3

I KNOW THIS IS DESPERATE, BUT I'M SENDING OUT A BOTTLE WITH A NOTE IN IT!
HOPEFULLY WE WON'T HAVE TO WAIT THAT LONG!
HONK
WHOA!! WHAT'S THAT?!
A BOAT!! WE'RE SAVED!!
THAT WAS ONE FAST TRAVELING BOTTLE!
OH, BROTHER!
AHOY! WHAT ARE YOU GUYS DOING WAY OUT HERE IN THE FISHING LANES?!
IT'S A LONG STORY! BUT WE SORTA DRIFTED OUT TO SEA!!
CAN YOU GIVE US A RIDE BACK?
IT'S BEEN A VERY SUCCESSFUL DAY FOR US, BUT WE'RE ABOUT TO HEAD BACK IN!
4

WE'RE PRETTY OVERLOADED WITH FISH! WE DON'T HAVE ROOM ONBOARD FOR YOU GUYS!

COULD YOU AT LEAST GIVE US A TOW?!
Hmm... THAT'S A THOUGHT!

MAYBE WE CAN WORK SOMETHING OUT!
AS LONG AS IT GETS US BACK TO SHORE!

AND SO...
'AS LONG AS IT GETS US BACK TO SHORE' YOU SAID!
I KNOW! DON'T REMIND ME!

I JUST DON'T KNOW IF I'LL EVER GET THIS FISH SMELL OFF MY ISLAND!!
QUIT YAKKIN' AND KEEP THOSE GULLS AWAY!!
ONLY AN HOUR MORE TO GO!
THE END

Archie in CHILL OUT!
WHAT A GREAT DAY FOR A CAMPING TRIP!
RIVERDALE NATIONAL PARK HAS SOME VERY BEAUTIFUL SPOTS!
DAN PARENT STORY & PENCILS
BOB SMITH INKS
GLENN WHITMORE COLORS
JACK MORELLI LETTERS
WOW!
CHECK OUT THIS OVERLOOK! LET'S SET UP HERE!
NO! WAIT--!
WE DON'T WANT TO CAMP HERE!
?!
1

THAT'S THE INFAMOUS "RIVERDALE RAMBLES"!
WHAT'S THAT?!

IT'S AN OLD BURIAL GROUND! HORRIBLE THINGS HAPPEN HERE!
IT SAYS SO RIGHT ON THIS WEBSITE!

LET'S SEE THAT!
UH, SEE? THERE YOU GO!
SWOOP
WELL, THIS SPOT IS PERFECT!
I SAY WE CAMP HERE!

I AGREE!
ME, TOO!
OKAY--IT'S YOUR FUNERALS!
SNICKER! NOW THAT I'VE PUT IT IN THEIR HEADS, IT'LL BE EASIER TO SCARE THEM!
2

LATER...
...AND WHEN THEY OPENED THE DOOR... THERE HE STOOD...
WITH NO HEAD!
AND A HOOK FOR A HAND!
EEEEEE!

WELL, G'NIGHT!
I DON'T KNOW IF I CAN SLEEP AFTER THAT STORY!

JUST SLEEP WITH ONE EYE OPEN AND YOU'LL BE FINE!
THANKS A LOT!

WHEN EVERYONE IS ASLEEP, I'LL SCARE THEM WITH MY HOOK HAND COSTUME!
UNTIL THEN...

SO...
TIME TO GET OUT INTO THE WOODS WITH MY SCARY GET-UP!
3

I'LL JUST GET SET UP OVER HERE...

HUH?! WHAT'S THAT OVER THERE?!

OHMIGOSH!
WHAT HAVE I STUMBLED UPON?!

STOP! I COMMAND YOU TO STOP!
IT'S COMING TOWARD ME!!

STOP!
THE POWER OF REGGIE COMPELS YOU!!
4

I'M DOOMED!! SOMEONE'S PUNISHING ME FOR STARTING THIS SCARY WOODS STUFF!!
WAIT--! IS THAT JUG-HEAD?!
JUGHEAD! STOP!

WHAT'S UP, REGGIE?
I HAVE TO GET MY PIZZA!

PIZZA?!
THAT'LL BE TWENTY BUCKS, PLEASE...
RAM
RAM PIZZA

WHY WOULDN'T YOU ANSWER ME?!
RAM
POP
RAM PIZZA
OH, SORRY, DUDE! HAD MY EAR-BUDS IN!

WANNA PIECE?
ANCHOVIES? NOW THAT'S SCARY!
END

Archie in ARCHIE APPLESEED

FRANCIS BONNET STORY | JEFF SHULTZ PENCILS | JIM AMASH INKS | GLENN WHITMORE COLORS | JACK MORELLI LETTERS

I'LL FIX THIS!!
YOU'LL BE THE MOST DESPISED PERSON IN RIVERDALE UNLESS YOU DO!

WHAT ARE WE GOING TO DO WITH THESE APPLES?
UNLESS YOU CAN EAT THEM ALL, JUGHEAD, I'LL PUT THEM IN MY BACKYARD!

AND SO...
I'M TIRED OF APPLES! LET'S GET A PIZZA!
FORGET IT! I STILL HAVE TO CLEAR THE APPLES OFF EVERY-ONE ELSE'S LAWNS!

I THINK I'LL HELP OL' ARCH OUT BY PLANTING A FEW SEEDS OF MY OWN!

LATER...
THAT'S THE LAST OF THEM! AND IT LOOKS LIKE MR. WEATHERBEE IS CALLING!
HE PROBABLY WANTS TO THANK US!
RING
PIZZA
2

ARCHIE!! WHY ARE THESE APPLES STILL ON MY LAWN?!!
BUT WE CLEANED THOSE OUT!
SOON...
I--I DONT UNDER-STAND...
WOK
WHAT'S NOT TO UNDERSTAND?!
CLEAN THIS UP!!

THEN...
HEY, CARROT-TOP! WHAT DO YOU THINK OF MY APPLE ANTICS?!
REGGIE?!
YOU PUT ALL THOSE APPLES BACK?!

YOU SHOULD'VE SEEN THE EXPRESSION ON YOUR FACE! THANKS FOR BEING A REAL SAUCE OF ENTERTAINMENT!

REGGIE AND HIS ROTTEN PRANKS!!
GUESS WE'LL JUST HAVE TO START GATHERING APPLES ANEW!
SLAM
3

NOW WE'RE FINALLY DONE!
YOUR BACKYARD LOOKS LIKE THE APPLE ALPS!

DAD--! LOOK OUT!
RUMBLE

WHY AM I BEING APPLE AMBUSHED?!

ARCHIE!! THESE APPLES HAVE GOT TO GO!
BUT WHERE?!

WE HAVE AN IDEA FOR YOUR APPLE ABUNDANCE!
BETTY! VERONICA! WHAT ARE YOU DOING HERE?!

IT WAS HARD NOT TO NOTICE THE GIANT MOUNTAIN OF APPLES IN YOUR YARD!
YOU SHOULD USE THEM IN AN APPLE FALL FESTIVAL!!
ACK!

THAT'S A GREAT IDEA!!
THEN LET'S GET STARTED!
4

I CAN'T BELIEVE HOW SUCCESSFUL OUR APPLE FALL FESTIVAL HAS BEEN!
YOU SHOULD MAKE THIS AN ANNUAL EVENT!
WE'LL CERTAINLY HAVE ENOUGH APPLES EVERY YEAR!

HEY, CARROT-TOP! HOW'D YOU GET STUCK WORKING THE TICKET BOOTH?
HE'S NOT JUST WORKING THE FESTIVAL, REGGIE-- HE'S RUNNING IT!

WHAT?!
LOOK AT ALL THE MONEY I'VE MADE SO FAR!

A TICKET TO GET IN IS USUALLY FIVE DOLLARS-- BUT FOR YOU, IT'S TEN!
I CAN'T BELIEVE THIS!

I'M GOING TO PLANT SOME PEAR TREES! GET READY FOR SOME COMPETITION IN FOUR YEARS!!
HE'S GOT A SERIOUS CASE OF APPLE ANIMOSITY!
END

Archie in UP ON THE HOUSETOP!

THANKS FOR JOINING ME, ARCHIE! I PLAN TO MAKE SURE THIS IS THE YEAR I FINALLY CATCH A GLIMPSE OF SANTA CLAUS!

I'M HERE FOR YOU, BETTY! I JUST HOPE THAT YOU'RE NOT DISAPPOINTED!

BILL GOLLIHER STORY | JEFF SHULTZ PENCILS | JIM AMASH INKS | GLENN WHITMORE COLORS | JACK MORELLI LETTERS

DO YOU WANT SOME MORE HOT CHOCOLATE?
NO THANKS! I THINK I'VE HAD ENOUGH!

LOOK AT THE TIME! DO YOU REALLY THINK HE'LL STILL SHOW?
OF COURSE-- HE'S SANTA!
yawn! NOW YOU'VE GOT ME DOING IT!

AND SO...
Z
JINGLE JINGLE

IT APPEARS THESE TWO TRIED TO WAIT UP FOR ME! I'D BETTER GET DOWN THE CHIMNEY AND GET TO WORK!
Z Z Z

HEY, PRANCER! THAT KID IS STANDING UP!
YOU'RE RIGHT! HE'S SLEEPWALKING TOWARDS THE EDGE OF THE ROOF! THAT LOOKS DANGEROUS!
2

HE'S GOING TO FALL OFF!
LET'S GET IT IN GEAR!

PLOP
Z Z Z
GOT HIM! ALL THOSE STUFFED ANIMALS SHOULD MAKE FOR A SOFT LANDING!

SOON...
SNORT
I DON'T KNOW WHAT YOU'RE TRYING TO TELL ME, BUT WE HAVE TO STAY ON SCHEDULE!
Z
CLOP
CLOP

HE'S IN FOR A SURPRISE!
YOU CAN'T ARGUE WITH THE BIG GUY, THOUGH!

LATER...
FINALLY! THE LAST STOP OF THE NIGHT! NOW TO GET THE GOODIES OUT OF --
Huh?! WHAT'S THIS?!
3

ARCHIE ANDREWS?! HOW DID HE WIND UP IN THERE?!
Z
SNORT

OF COURSE! THAT'S WHAT YOU GUYS WERE TRYING TO TELL ME EARLIER!
Z

WE HAVE TO GET HIM BACK TO THAT ROOFTOP WITH BETTY! NEXT STOP, RIVERDALE! AGAIN!
ZZZ
SNORT SNORT

OH, GOOD! BETTY'S STILL ASLEEP! NOW TO PLACE HIM BACK AT HER SIDE!
Z
ZZZZ

THAT DOES IT! LET'S CALL IT A CHRISTMAS!
FINALLY!
ZZZ
4

:YAWN!: ARCHIE! WAKE UP!
HUH? WHAT?!

DARN IT! WE FELL ASLEEP AND MISSED HIM!
HOW DO YOU KNOW HE WAS HERE?!

BECAUSE LOOK! HE LEFT US EACH A GIFT!
SAY, YOU'RE RIGHT!

BUT THAT'S THE LEAST HE COULD HAVE DONE!
WHY DO YOU SAY THAT?

AFTER ALL, I DID SPEND AN ENTIRE BORING NIGHT ON A ROOFTOP WAITING FOR HIM!
END

BETTY & VERONICA

Betty and Veronica in PUSSYCATS for HIRE!

RIVERDALE WINTERFEST

RIVERDALE'S *WINTERFEST* IS UNDERWAY!

IT'S AWESOME THAT *JOSIE* AND THE *PUSSYCATS* ARE GOING TO PERFORM!

THIS WEEKEND! Josie AND THE PUSSYCATS

DAN **PARENT** STORY & PENCILS

BOB **SMITH** INKS

GLENN **WHITMORE** COLORS

JACK **MORELLI** LETTERS

OH, LOOK! THEY'RE REHEARSING!
YEAH-- BAY-BEE--
--I'VE GOT TO SEE YOU!!
KRIK
!
OUCH!
FLING
BONK
JOSIE AND THE PUSSYCATS
BONK
MELODY! WHAT'S WRONG?!
I-IT'S MY WRIST! I THINK I SPRAINED IT!
2

ARE YOU OK, VALERIE?
VALERIE?!

THAT DRUMSTICK LEFT YOU WITH QUITE A *BUMP!*
TROUBLE IN PUSSYCAT LAND, IT LOOKS LIKE.

SO...
BETTY, THE GIRLS ARE OUT OF *COMMISSION!*
WOULD YOU AND VERONICA LIKE TO TAKE THEIR PLACES?

BETTY AND VERONICA AS *PUSSY-CATS?!*
I LIKE IT!!

BETTY'S DRUM LESSONS HAVE REALLY PAID OFF!
JOSIE AND THE PUSSYCATS
THE NIGHT OF THE CONCERT...
LOOKING AND SOUNDING GOOD!
WHAT'S UP WITH VERONICA?
SHE DOESN'T LOOK TOO GOOD!
URK! I THINK THAT TAMALÉ I ATE ISN'T AGREEING WITH ME!
FLING
MRK!
BONK
RING
VERONICA! ARE YOU OKAY?!
I THINK I'M THE VICTIM OF A BAD TAMALÉ!
WHAT DO WE DO?!
I GUESS WE CARRY ON WITHOUT HER!
4

UH-OH! I HAD ONE OF THOSE TAMALES, TOO!
I THINK I'M GONNA HURL!
BLURP

MRF!
I GUESS I'LL HAVE TO SHUT THIS DOWN.!

JOSIE! WE HAVE AN IDEA!
OKAY! I'M LISTENING...

SO...
WELCOME OUR GUEST PUSSYCATS-- ARCHIE AND JUGHEAD!!

I LIKE THE CAT EARS!
THEY WORK ON YOU!
UH-OH! I DON'T FEEL SO GOOD...
END

Betty and Veronica in Hansel & Gretel Inc.

Once upon a time there were two HOME IMPROVEMENT business partners named HANSEL & GRETEL...

WHAT A ROTTEN JOB! SELLING HOME IMPROVEMENT PACKAGES TO THE FOREST FOLK!

HANSEL, I'M SO TURNED AROUND THAT I'VE BEEN LEAVING A TRAIL OF BREAD CRUMBS TO FIND OUR WAY BACK TO OUR WAGON IN THE CLEARING!

H & G HOME IMPROVEMENTS

BILL GOLLIHER STORY

DAN PARENT PENCILS

JIM AMASH INKS

GLENN WHITMORE COLORS

JACK MORELLI LETTERS

HEY, TRY A PIECE OF THE SIDING! IT'S GINGERBREAD!
MMM! SURE BEATS CHEWING ON VINYL!

NIBBLE, NIBBLE, LITTLE HOME IMPROVEMENT PEOPLE! WHO'S THAT NIBBLING ON MY HOUSE?
SORRY, MA'AM, BUT WE COULDN'T RESIST! I MUST SAY YOUR HOME IS DELICIOUS!

LET ME PRESENT OUR CARD...
H AND G HOME IMPROVEMENTS!
H&G HOME IMPROVEMENTS
DO COME IN AND TELL ME WHAT YOU WOULD SUGGEST!
FIRST OFF, I WOULDN'T RECOMMEND THE SOLAR PANELS! THEY WOULD WREAK HAVOC ON YOUR ICING!

HOW LONG HAVE YOU LIVED HERE? MAYBE YOUR CANDY COULD USE SOME UPDATING!
NO, I WOULD SAY EVERYTHING IS STILL RELATIVELY FRESH!

I WOULD SAY SO! I JUST ASSUMED BECAUSE YOU HAD THAT CLOAK ON, YOU WERE OLDER!
THANKS!
DO TELL ME ALL ABOUT YOUR DEAR LITTLE PROJECTS!
2

HOW ABOUT WINDOWS? DO YOU HAVE ANY SAMPLE ONES?
BACK IN THE WAGON!

WHY DON'T YOU HAVE YOUR PARTNER BE A DEAR AND GO FETCH THEM?
YOU HEARD THE LADY, GRETEL! WE MIGHT HAVE A SALE HERE!

FINE! IF I DON'T COME BACK, I'M HOPELESSLY LOST BECAUSE SOME-ONE ATE MY BREAD-CRUMBS!
COMPLAIN, COMPLAIN! IT'S IMPOSSIBLE TO FIND GOOD HELP IN THESE DARK AGES!
H&G
HOME IMPROVEMENTS

NOW THAT WE'RE ALONE, MAYBE YOU COULD TAKE A LOOK AT MY STOVE!
GLAD TO! I'M TOTALLY AT HOME IN THE KITCHEN!

OH, YEAH! WE COULD DO WONDERS WITH THIS PLACE! ALL STAINLESS STEEL!
REALLY? COULD YOU TAKE A CLOSE LOOK AT MY OVEN AND TELL ME WHAT'S WRONG WITH IT?

PLEASE, TAKE AN EVEN CLOSER LOOK!
LADY, IF I GOT ANY CLOSER I'D BE IN IT!
SO YOU WOULD!
Heh-Heh!!
3

LATER...
URF! HOW COME I HAD TO GET THE WINDOWS OUT OF THE WAGON?!
PSST! HEY YOU, GIRLIE! OVER HERE!

WHO ARE YOU?!
LET'S SAY A CONCERNED NEIGHBOR! THE LADY THAT LIVES IN THAT HOUSE IS A WITCH!

SHE SEEMED FRIENDLY ENOUGH TO ME!
NO! I MEAN A BROOMSTICK-RIDING, SPELL-CASTING WITCH! IF YOU LEFT YOUR FRIEND IN THERE, HE COULD BE IN TROUBLE!
I WAS CONCERNED SHE MIGHT BE TOO FRIENDLY WITH HIM WHILE I WAS GONE!
LET'S TAKE A PEEK INSIDE!

EVERYTHING IS FINE! SHE'S JUST CARRYING A LIFE-SIZED GINGER-BREAD MAN WITH ORANGE HAIR!
ULP!

SHE MUST'VE BAKED MY GINGER PARTNER INTO A REAL GINGER-BREAD MAN!
SEE! I TOLD YOU SO!
4

WE'VE GOT TO RESCUE HIM!
DON'T WORRY! I'VE BEEN DYING TO EAT MY WAY INSIDE THERE!

CHOMP CHOMP
YOU DID IT! HAND OVER HANSEL, YOU WITCH!
HUH?!

I'M RIGHT HERE! WHAT'S THE BIG DEAL?!
Y-YOU'RE COOKING?!
KISS THE CHEF

YES! WE'RE BAKING A NEW ADDITION TO THE HOUSE! COMPLETE WITH A LIFE-SIZED GINGERBREAD MAN OF YOURS TRULY!
?
ISN'T HE CUTE?!
HE TOLD ME HE WAS AT HOME IN THE KITCHEN, BUT I HAD NO IDEA!
KISS THE CHEF

SOON...
OKAY! WE'VE GOT THE NEW WING READY TO GO UP!
HOLD ON! THE DEMOLITION MAN IS STILL WORKING ON THE OLD ONE!
CHOMP GNAW CHOMP
AWWW! YOU GUYS ARE THE SWEETEST!!
MUNCH MUNCH MUNCH
The END

Betty and Veronica in What if Betty & Veronica were Super-Geniuses?

WHAT AMAZING SCIENTIFIC DISCOVERY ARE MY TWO FELLOW GENIUSES WORKING ON TODAY?

SO GLAD YOU ASKED, DILTON!

WE'VE POOLED OUR MENTAL RESOURCES TO COME UP WITH AN AMAZING COMPUTER PROGRAM!

b&v LABS

BILL GOLLIHER STORY | DAN PARENT PENCILS | BOB SMITH INKS | GLENN WHITMORE COLORS | JACK MORELLI LETTERS

BEEP BEEP
GASP!
OH, DEAR! IT APPEARS THE RESULTS FOR EACH OF US ARE THE SAME...

ARCHIE ANDREWS!
ARCHIE?! ARE YOU SURE YOUR PRO-GRAMMING WAS CORRECT?

THERE'S NO MISTAKE! AND OF COURSE THERE WILL BE NO COMPETITION, EITHER!
OF COURSE NOT! BECAUSE I'M THE ONE WHO WILL WIND UP WITH HIM!

THAT'S NOT WHAT I MEANT! THIS SHALL BE A BATTLE OF WITS!
OVER THE WITLESS! ARCHIE SHOULD DECIDE WHO HE WANTS!

YOU CAN'T BE SERIOUS! DO YOU KNOW WHAT HIS IQ IS?!
WE KNOW WHAT'S BEST FOR HIM!

SO...
ARCHIE-- TO CONFIRM THAT YOU ARE THE RIGHT CHOICE FOR ME, WEAR THIS DEVICE WHILE I KISS YOU AND MONITOR YOUR REACTION!
OKAY! ANYTHING TO ADVANCE SCIENCE!
2

WAIT! I WAS ABOUT TO DO A SIMILAR EXPERIMENT ON HIM WITH THAT SAME EQUIPMENT!
EASY, GIRL! I WAS HERE FIRST! YOU CAN GO NEXT!
THIS IS THE STRANGEST DATE I'VE EVER HEARD OF!

SOON...
THE DATA IS IN! SHALL WE GO MONITOR THE RESULTS?
MOST DEFINITELY!

THERE'S A DEFINITE LEVEL OF INTEREST, BUT NOT AS OVER-WHELMING AS I'D HOPED!
YES, IT SEEMS OUR REACTIONS WERE A TIE AS FAR AS HE'S CONCERNED!
BEEP

GUESS THIS CALLS FOR DESPERATE MEASURES--LIKE MY LITTLE BLACK EVENING LAB COAT!
AND MY PERIODIC TABLE WORKOUT SUIT!
HUBBA! HUBBA!
Co
Ni
D
V
Re
Ce
Ti
Pt
Pm
3

A HIGHER REACTION, BUT STILL NOT WHAT I WAS LOOKING FOR!
I AGREE!
BEEP BEEP
Co Ni V Re Ce Ti Pt Pm

HOLD ON! SOMETHING IS SENDING THE RESULTS OFF THE CHARTS!
NOW THAT'S THE REACTION WE'RE HOPING FOR! LET'S FIND THE SOURCE!
BEEP BEEP BEEP

JUGHEAD HAS THE DEVICE ON?!
SORRY, GIRLS! I JUST FIGURED I'D HAVE JUG TRY OUT YOUR HELMET-THINGY WHILE EATING!

AMAZING! I'VE NEVER SEEN SUCH A REACTION!
IT'S THE LEVEL OF PASSION THAT WE'RE LOOKING FOR--BUT IT'S OVER A HAMBURGER!!
MUNCH

LET'S USE POP'S SPECIALS BLACKBOARD TO DOUBLE CHECK OUR CALCULATIONS ON ARCHIE! MAYBE WE MISSED SOMETHING!
SPECIAL
THAT'S ALWAYS A GOOD IDEA!
Re Ta Bh At Np Se Yb

BEEP BEEP BEEP
Whoa! WHAT'S GOING ON NOW?! THE READINGS ARE EVEN FURTHER OFF THE SCALE!!
BEEEP
WHAT ARE THEY SERVING JUGHEAD NOW?!
4

IT'S NOT JUGHEAD! DILTON IS WEARING THE HELMET AND HE'S LOOKING AT US!
I JUST LOVE WHEN GIRLS DO COMPUTATIONS!
APPARENTLY DILTON IS THE ONE WE SHOULD BE PURSUING!
I GUESS WE SHOULD HAVE LISTED HIM IN OUR DATABASE TO START WITH!
THUMPA-THUMPA-THUMP
WE JUST ASSUMED HE WAS TOO BUSY WITH HIS INVENTIONS TO NOTICE US!
YES--NOW DO TELL US MORE ABOUT THAT CLONING IDEA YOU HAD!
?!
WHAT ABOUT ME?! WHAT DOES THE FUTURE HOLD FOR ME?
Hmmmm...
POP'S
I GUESS WE COULD ALWAYS SEE HOW EXCITED YOU GET OVER A CHEESEBURGER!
BEEP BEEP BEEP
The END

Betty and Veronica in

WHAT IF... Betty & Veronica HAD NEVER MET UNTIL... NOW?

THE LOBBY OF LODGE INDUSTRIES...

HOLD THAT ELEVATOR!!

SURE THING! ARE YOU HERE FOR THE INTERVIEW, TOO?

BILL GOLLIHER STORY

DAN PARENT PENCILS

JIM AMASH INKS

GLENN WHITMORE COLORS

JACK MORELLI LETTERS

GOOD LUCK WITH THAT... WHAT'S HAPPENING? THE ELEVATOR STOPPED!!
SKREEE
THUNK
I THINK WE MAY BE STUCK!

THIS IS A BUSY BUILDING! I'M SURE SOMEONE WILL NOTICE SOON!
EEEEKK!! NONE OF THESE BUTTONS ARE DOING ANY-THING!
TAP TAP TAP

I'M CLAUSTROPHOBIC! I'M CALLING MY FATHER!
I THINK WE JUST NEED TO STAY CALM!

OF ALL TIMES FOR MY PHONE BATTERY TO BE DEAD! GIVE ME YOUR PHONE!
I WILL! BUT HOLD ON A SEC!

I JUST LOOKED UP WHAT TO DO IF YOU'RE STUCK INSIDE AN ELEVATOR! IT SAYS...
SCREAM YOUR HEAD OFF?!!
2

NO! THE MOST IMPORTANT THING TO DO IS TO STAY CALM! CAN YOU THINK OF SOMETHING SOOTHING?
CREDIT CARDS!

NOW--TAKE A DEEP BREATH AND RELAX YOURSELF! IT'S HARD FOR YOUR MIND TO BE IN A PANIC WHEN YOUR BODY IS RELAXED!
Whoosh!

NOW WE SIMPLY PUSH THE CALL BUTTON TO LET THE PROPER PEOPLE KNOW WE HAVE A PROBLEM!
YES? IS EVERYONE OKAY?

WE REALIZE YOUR ELEVATOR IS STUCK... WE SHOULD HAVE YOU OUT OF THERE SHORTLY!
...AND TELL MY FATHER--
--THAT VERONICA IS SAFE!

MS. LODGE?! YOU'RE IN THERE?! WE'LL HAVE YOU OUT EVEN FASTER!!
IT LOOKS LIKE I GOT TRAPPED WITH THE RIGHT PERSON!

SOON...
CREAKK
THE ELEVATOR! IT'S MOVING AGAIN!
3

VERONICA, DEAR! YOU'RE SAFE--AND AMAZINGLY CALM!
YES, THANKS TO THIS GIRL! I COULDN'T HAVE SURVIVED WITHOUT HER!

THANK YOU, YOUNG LADY! WHAT'S YOUR NAME?
COOPER--BETTY COOPER! AND THERE'S ACTUALLY A FUNNY STORY OF WHY I'M HERE...

LATER, AT POP'S...
AND THAT'S HOW I GOT THE INTERN-SHIP!
WOW! AND YOU MET HIRAM LODGE AND HIS DAUGHTER!

I HEAR SHE GOES TO ONE OF THOSE FANCY CROSSTOWN PRIVATE ACADEMIES!
I'M NOT SURPRISED!
THERE YOU ARE!

VERONICA LODGE!
BETTY COOPER! I'M GLAD I FOUND YOU! I GOT YOUR ADDRESS FROM YOUR APPLICATION, AND YOUR MOM SAID YOU MIGHT BE HERE!
WHY WERE YOU LOOKING FOR ME?
4

TO THANK YOU AGAIN FOR GETTING ME THROUGH THAT ELEVATOR ORDEAL!
Oh, IT WAS NOTHING!
AFTER THAT ADVENTURE, I WAS THINKING WE NEED TO GET TO KNOW EACH OTHER BETTER! THIS COULD BE JUST THE BEGINNING!
Ahem!
Oh, EXCUSE ME! LET ME INTRODUCE YOU TO MY BOY-FRIEND, ARCHIE ANDREWS!
ARCHIE, Huh?
PLEASED TO MEET YOU!
Duh... AND YOU, TOO!
?
ON SECOND THOUGHT, I THINK WE MAY ALL NEED TO GET TO KNOW EACH OTHER BETTER!
THAT SOUNDS WONDERFUL!
I HOPE SHE DOESN'T REGRET THIS!
THE END

Betty and Veronica in The Best Summer Ever!

SCHOOL'S OUT!

NOW FOR A FEW MONTHS OF REST AND RELAXATION!

NO! WE ALWAYS WASTE OUR SUMMERS AND THEN IT'S TIME FOR SCHOOL AGAIN!

BETTY'S RIGHT! WE NEED TO COMMIT TO MAKE THIS OUR BEST SUMMER EVER!

BILL GOLLIHER STORY | DAN PARENT PENCILS | BOB SMITH INKS | GLENN WHITMORE COLORS | JACK MORELLI LETTERS

NEXT DAY...
I'LL GO EASY ON YOU GUYS! WE'LL JUST DO TEN MILES ON THE RIVERDALE TRAIL!
TEN MILES IS EASY? WHAT DO YOU CALL DIFFICULT?!
THE LAST ONE HAS TO BUY THE REFRESHMENTS AFTERWARDS!
GASP!
A-ARE YOU KIDDING?!
Instant-gram
Betty Cooper
SLURP
Thanks for picking up the post-cycling tab, Reggie!
THAT WAS A BLAST!
WHAT'S NEXT?!
THAT WOULD BE MY PICK--WHITEWATER RAFTING ON THE PICKENS RIVER!
AND SO!
JUGHEAD, WHAT'S WITH THE FLOAT?!
I PLAN TO BE DOUBLY SAFE!
WOW! THIS IS EXCITING!
YEAH! I DON'T THINK I HAVE A DRY SPOT LEFT!
SPOOSH
2

SPLASH
NOW THERE'S NOTHING DRY FOR SURE!
Instant-gram
Veronica Lodge
Making a splash in the Pickens River with my besties!
VERONICA--LET'S MAKE IT YOUR TURN! WHAT DO YOU HAVE IN STORE FOR US?
BELIEVE IT OR NOT... CAMPING!
AND SO...
CAMPING WITH A BUTLER?! I THINK THIS IS MORE LIKE "GLAM-PING"!
YOUR S'MORE, MADAM!
NOW I'LL GO TURN DOWN THE SLEEPING BAGS!
IT'S THE ONLY WAY TO ROUGH IT!
Instant-gram
Betty Cooper
Camping Lodge-style! LOVE IT!
3

ARCHIE--YOU'RE UP! WHAT WOULD YOU LIKE US TO DO?
A FULL DAY HIKE TO THE TOP OF MOUNT PICKENS!

THAT'S A HAUL!
YES! BUT THIS IS...
I KNOW... OUR "BEST SUMMER EVER"--
--AND THE MOST TIRING ONE!

HIKE DAY...
GROWL!
JUG! IF YOUR STOMACH IS GROWLING, HAVE A SNACK!

MY STOMACH'S NOT GROWLING!
THEN WHAT...
GRRRR...
EEP! A BEAR!

TAKE THE EXPRESS LANE TO THE TOP, EVERYONE!
YOU DON'T HAVE TO TELL ME TWICE!!
?
KLAK

WE'RE HERE... GASP! HUFF!
OH, NO! I DROPPED MY PHONE BACK THERE!
PICKENS PEAK 4,101 ft.
I'LL HAVE TO FIND IT ON THE WAY BACK DOWN!
4

Instant-gram
Betty Cooper
Looks like someone took a selfie after I dropped my phone!
JUGHEAD, I MUST SAY YOUR CHOICE WAS THE BEST WAY TO WRAP UP OUR SUMMER!
YEAH--A RELAXING DAY AT THE WATER PARK!
NOTHING LIKE A LAZY RIVER!
ESPECIALLY WHEN YOU'RE LAZY!
I THINK WE CAN SAY THIS IS A SUMMER WE WILL ALWAYS REMEMBER!
YEAH! BUT WHAT ABOUT NEXT SUMMER?
WHAT DO YOU MEAN?
SOMEHOW WE HAVE TO TOP IT NEXT TIME AROUND! ANY IDEAS?
WHY DON'T WE ASK OUR FRIENDS ON SOCIAL MEDIA? MAYBE THEY HAVE SOME IDEAS!
Instant-gram
Veronica Lodge
Any ideas for next summer? In the meantime...THE END!
THE END

Betty and Veronica in Water Songs!

PICKENS PARK
RIVERDALE Mermaid DAY

THE BIG DAY IS HERE!

STORY by: JAMIE L. ROTANTE

DAN PARENT PENCILS | JIM AMASH INKS | GLENN WHITMORE COLORS

JACK MORELLI : LETTERS

MONADE
WELL, WE HAD TO START SOMEWHERE! AND IF SELLING LEMONADE AS SCALLYWAGS IS IT, SO BE IT! IT'S A PIRATE'S LIFE FOR ME!
YARR.

HI, ARCHIE! HI, JUGHEAD!
IT'S COOL THAT YOU GUYS ARE WORKING HERE! DID YOU SEE THIS YEAR'S NEW MERMAID QUEEN?
S
DID YOU ALSO SEE THIS YEAR'S NEW CLAMS CASINO STAND?

WOW, COULD YOU IMAGINE GETTING THAT ROLE? THE MERMAID QUEEN IS ALWAYS SO MAGICAL!
COULD YOU IMAGINE WANTING TO EAT CLAMS CASINO AT A FESTIVAL?
GANG WAY!!

MAKE WAY FOR the Mermaid QUEEN!

YES, YES! MOVE ASIDE!
THE QUEEN HAS ARRIVED!
2

Oh, HELLO WENCHES. I'LL TAKE A LEMONADE... ON THE HOUSE.
HELLO, CHERYL.
TUT-TUT! THAT'S QUEEN CORALIA TO YOU!
YUCK!
TOO BITTER... JUST LIKE YOU TWO!
TA!
JUST IGNORE HER, RONNIE!
BUT SHE GETS ALL THE ATTENTION! SHE GETS WAITED ON HAND AND, ER... FIN. SHE GETS THE BEST COSTUME!!
YEAH, FOR ONE DAY ONLY! LET'S NOT GIVE HER EVEN MORE OF A REASON TO LET IT GET TO HER HEAD!
ARRRGH!
THAT'S THE PIRATE SPIRIT!
CAN I GET AN EXTRA DROP OF SUGAR IN THERE?
Ohhh, A DROP OF SUGAR WON'T DO YA ANY HARM!
BLIMEY, BETTY!
Huh?!
KEEP SINGING!
3

Oh, SQUEEZE FRESH LEMONS, PIRATES, SQUEEZE THE FRESH LEMONS...
SQUEEZE THE FRESH LEMONS, PIRATES, SQUEEZE THE FRESH LEMONS! GIVE ME SOME TIME TO SQUEEZE THE FRESH LEMONS!
WHAT WILL WE DO WITH A THIRSTY SAILOR? WHAT WILL WE DO WITH A THIRSTY SAILOR? WHAT WILL WE DO WITH A THIRSTY SAILOR--
--IN THE AFTERNOON?!
Queen Coralia's Fairy Tale
Oh, WILL MY PRINCE EVER FIIIIIND ME--
HEY--WHERE ARE YOU ALL GOING?!
WHAT WILL WE DO WITH A THIRSTY SAILOR? WHAT WILL WE DO WITH A THIRSTY SAILOR? WHAT WILL WE DO WITH A THIRSTY SAILOR--IN THE AFTERNOON?!
THIS MUST BE STOPPED!
4

HEAVE AWAY, HAUL AWAY!!
HAUL AWAY, Oh HEAR ME SIIIING!
ARRRGHH!!
GREAT JOB, CHERYL! NOW EVERYONE'S LEAVING!
?!
Huh?!
WOOAAH
THAT VOICE!
OOOAAAAHWOOOO
IT'S LIKE MAGIC!
SOMEONE HAD TO SAVE THE DAY!
END

Betty and Veronica in CHEERS TO YOU!

RIVERDALE! RIVERDALE!

RAH! RAH! RAH!

DAN PARENT STORY & PENCILS

BOB SMITH INKS

GLENN WHITMORE COLORS

JACK MORELLI LETTERS

BETTY'S AWESOME AT IT.!
IF YOU SAY SO!

THEN YOU WON'T HAVE TO WORRY ABOUT BEING ON TELEVISION.!
WHAT ARE YOU TALKING ABOUT?

THE REALITY SHOW "CHEERS TO YOU" IS COMING HERE!
BIG DEAL! WHO WANTS TO BE ON THAT SHOW ANYWAY?!

NATIONAL T.V.! THIS COULD BE MY BIG BREAK!

SO...
HOW AM I DOING, COACH VELMA?!
TO PUT IT SIMPLY...

...DON'T GIVE UP YOUR DAY JOB!
WHAT?!! I HIRED YOU TO MAKE ME A WORLD CLASS CHEERLEADER!
2

OKAY--BUT IT'S GOING TO REQUIRE A LOT MORE PRACTICE!
AND A MIRACLE!
AT THE BIG REALITY SHOW TRY-OUTS...
SIS-BOOM-BAH!

RIIIIIVERDALE--YEAH!
EXCELLENT! NICE JOB, MISS COOPER!

NEXT UP IS VERONICA LODGE!
WHERE IS SHE?
Cheers TO YOU!

WHAT'S WITH THE SMOKE?
AND BLINDING LIGHTS?

LOOKS LIKE SHE'S MAKING AN ENTRANCE!
3

WOW! HER NAME IN LIGHTS! THAT MUST HAVE COST A PRETTY PENNY!
VERONICA
PLEASE START, MISS LODGE!

R-I-V-E-R-D-A-L-E!!

WHAT DOES IT SPELL?!

FLIP
WHOMP

LOOKS LIKE IT SPELLS... DISASTER!
GOOD THING I I GOT PAID UP FRONT!

FORGET IT!!
YOU PEOPLE DON'T APPRECIATE REAL ART!!
4

THAT AFTER-NOON...
I THOUGHT I'D FIND YOU HERE!
I SUPPOSE YOU'RE HERE TO GLOAT ABOUT WINNING?

I DIDN'T GET ON THE SHOW EITHER!
WHAT? BUT YOU WERE AWESOME! AND A NATURAL!
BUT I'M NO JUGHEAD!
WHAT?!

THAT'S RIGHT! HE GOT UP THERE AND DID THIS AMAZING ROUTINE!
HE FOUND OUT THAT THE SHOW IS SPONSORED BY TACO HUT, SO HE THINKS HE CAN GET FREE FOOD FOR LIFE!

HE WOWED THEM ALL BECAUSE OF HIS GLUTTONOUS DREAMS!
AARGHH!
I EXPECT TO LOSE TO YOU SOMETIMES! THAT I CAN HANDLE!
BUT TO LOSE TO JUGHEAD?! THAT'S A BRIDGE TOO FAR!!
END

FRANCIS BONNET STORY
The FAB K-BROS PENCILS
JIM AMASH INKS
GLENN WHITMORE COLORS
JACK MORELLI LETTERS

THESE MIGHT GO WELL WITH OUR COSTUMES FOR YOUR HALLOWEEN PARTY TONIGHT, VERONICA!

BETTY, NONE OF THOSE COMPARE TO THE BEAUTIFUL JEWELRY THAT **SHE'S** WEARING!

Oh, DO YOU LIKE MY **NECKLACE** AND **BRACELET**?

BAT WINGS

THEY'VE BEEN IN MY FAMILY FOR **GENERATIONS**!

Betty and Veronica IN CURSETUME PARTY

THIS JEWELRY IS BEAUTIFUL!
IT WAS SO NICE OF HER TO GIVE THEM TO US!
!

WE SHOULD PICK UP THE DECORATIONS FOR THE PARTY!
NOW, WHERE ARE MY CAR KEYS?

Oh, NO! MY KEYS!

HERE, USE THE FLASHLIGHT ON MY PHONE!
NO THANKS! I'D RATHER NOT SEE WHAT I'M REACHING INTO!

MY PURSE!
I DIDN'T HEAR ABOUT RAIN IN TODAY'S FORECAST!
SPLOOSH

WE HAVE TO GO AFTER THAT CAT!
LEAD THE WAY!
2

THERE HE GOES!
BETTY, WAIT! RUNNING UNDER A LADDER IS BAD LUCK!
WE'VE HAD NOTHING BUT BAD LUCK SINCE WE PUT ON THIS JEWELRY!
AT LEAST THE ORANGE WORKS FOR HALLOWEEN!
WOMP

THAT CAT IS FAST! LET'S GET MY CAR AND SEE IF WE CAN CATCH UP!
I MIGHT NEED A SMALL NAPKIN TO COVER YOUR SEATS!

MY CAR NEVER HAD TROUBLE STARTING BEFORE!
I'M BEGINNING TO THINK THIS JEWELRY IS CURSED!
R-R-R-R-R

I'M BEGINNING TO THINK YOU'RE RIGHT!
HALLOWEEN DECOR
HALLOWEEN DECOR
SCREEEEE

AHHHHH!!

WE NEED TO GET RID OF THIS CURSED JEWELRY!
RIVERDALE TENNIS CLUB

BY GETTING THEM AS FAR AWAY AS POSSIBLE!
BOP

THEY CAME BACK!
YOU TRY THIS TIME!

TRAMPOLINES "R" US!
POP'S
BOING
THIS CAN'T BE HAPPENING!

THIRD TIME IS THE CHARM!
THE UNLUCKY CHARM!

LOOK! IT'S THE CAT!!
DROP MY PURSE, YOU THIEF!!
4

HE'S DROPPED IT!
THAT'S THE BEST LUCK WE'VE HAD ALL DAY! THE CURSE MUST BE GONE!
THANK GOODNESS!
WE'D BETTER FINISH PREPARING FOR THE PARTY!
THIS IS THE LAST DECORATION!
AND NOT A MOMENT TOO SOON! IT SOUNDS LIKE WE HAVE OUR FIRST GUEST!
RING
LOOK! I FOUND THE BRACELET AND NECKLACE THAT YOU TWO ACCIDENTALLY THREW AWAY! TALK ABOUT LUCKY!
KICKK
WELL THAT'S THE LAST TIME I EVER DO SOMETHING NICE FOR THEM!
END

Betty and Veronica IN Leaf ME ALONE!
BETTY! WHAT ARE YOU DOING? I THOUGHT WE WERE GOING TO THE MALL!
I CAN'T! I HAVE TO CLEAN THE LEAVES OFF THE LAWN!
DAN PARENT STORY & PENCILS
BOB SMITH INKS
GLENN WHITMORE COLORS
JACK MORELLI LETTERS
CAN'T IT WAIT UNTIL LATER?
NO! I PROMISED MY MOM THAT I'D DO IT DAYS AGO!
ISN'T THAT WHAT GARDENERS ARE FOR?
I'M AFRAID OUR GARDENER IS OFF THIS WEEK!
1

OKAY, WELL LET ME KNOW IF AND WHEN YOU FINISH!
THERE ARE SALES TO BE CONQUERED!

YOU COULD STAY AND HELP ME!
GIGGLE! YOU'RE TOO FUNNY!

THAT POOR GIRL! SHE'S ALL WORK AND NO FUN!

WOOSH
WHAT THE--?!
SORRY, RON!

WHAT ARE YOU IMBECILES DOING?!
WE'RE HAVING A LEAF BLOWER RACE! WE SAW THIS ON YOUTUBE!
WOOSH
2

WOW! NOW I'VE SEEN IT ALL!
GOTTA KEEP MOVING! JUG'S GETTING AHEAD OF ME!
GIVE IT UP, ARCH!
I HAVEN'T EVEN STARTED YET!
WATCH OUT FOR THAT POTHOLE!
NICE TRY, JUG--
KA-PWUMP
THWAPP
WHAT THE--?!
KEEP IT GOING, BETTY!
WOOSH
NOW YOU'RE IN THE RACE!
3

RACE?!
RACE FOR WHAT?
GIVE IT UP, BETTY!
THIS ISN'T A GIRL'S SPORT!
I'M NOT SURE THIS IS EVEN A SPORT...
BUT DON'T TELL ME WHAT I CAN AND CANNOT DO!!
WOOSH
GIGGLE!
THIS IS KINDA FUN!
I WONDER HOW I TURN THIS THING AROUND?
WHAT THE--?!
HAS THE WORLD GONE MAD?!
SHWAPP
4

HI, RON!
BETTY! STOP THIS CRAZY THING!
OKAY! I NEED TO SHUT OFF THE LEAF BLOWER--
--BUT THE SWITCH IS JAMMED!
OH, GREAT! WE'RE NOW HEADED INTO TRAFFIC!
HOLD ON! I THINK I CAN STEER US AWAY!
DOWNTO
RIVER
SEE? WE'VE AVOIDED THAT TRAFFIC!
LOOK OUT FOR THAT WALL!!
KRASH
OOF! NOW I'M SEEING STARS!
LOOK ON THE BRIGHT SIDE, RON! THERE'S THE MALL!
MALL
THE END

Betty and Veronica in

HOLIDAY LIGHTS!

IS EVERYTHING SET FOR OUR CHRISTMAS PARTY TONIGHT, VERONICA?

YOU BET, BETTY! IT SHOULD BE QUITE THE SHINDIG WITH A KILLER LIGHT DISPLAY ACROSS THE ESTATE!

NOT TO MENTION ALL THE OTHER ACTIVITIES I HAVE PLANNED!

BILL GOLLIHER STORY & PENCILS | JIM AMASH INKS | GLENN WHITMORE COLORS | JACK MORELLI LETTERS

I'M NOT PUNCHING ANYONE! THIS IS A CHRISTMAS PARTY!
NO, MOOSE! DECK THE HALLS MEANS--
BETTY, JUST DROP IT!

TONI! KEVIN! WELCOME TO OUR HOLIDAY PARTY!
OF COURSE! WE WOULDN'T MISS IT!

WE EVEN BROUGHT OUR WHITE ELEPHANT GIFTS!
BRING THEM ON IN! THE SNACKS ARE ALMOST READY!

DID SOMEONE SAY SNACKS?
JUGHEAD AND I ARE HERE!
ARCHIE! IT WOULDN'T BE A PARTY WITHOUT YOU!

SOON!
WELCOME TO THE PARTY, EVERYONE! I'M GOING TO THROW THE SWITCH AND PUT ON THE LODGE LIGHT DISPLAY!
YOU MAY WANT TO NOW PUT ON YOUR PROVIDED SUNGLASSES!
ON
OFF
2

HERE GOES!
KLIK
OOOOOO!!
ON
OFF

BUT THEN...
BZATT!
WHAT'S HAPPENED?!!
THE POWER WENT OUT! THE LIGHT DISPLAY MUST HAVE BEEN TOO MUCH!

THE WHOLE NEIGHBOR-HOOD SEEMS TO BE OUT! RIGHT, DILTON?
I THINK THAT YOUR ELECTRICIANS HAVE MISCALCULATED THE AMOUNT OF POWER YOUR DISPLAY REQUIRES! IT CAUSED QUITE A SURGE!

HOW CAN WE HAVE A PARTY WITH NO POWER?!
WE'LL HAVE TO POSTPONE IT!!
3

WE'VE GOT FOOD! LET'S GO AHEAD AND HAVE THIS PARTY!
YEAH-- THEY WERE HAVING CHRISTMAS PARTIES LONG BEFORE ELECTRICITY!
EVERYONE LIGHT UP YOUR PHONES WHILE I GRAB SOME CANDLES! VERONICA, WHY DON'T YOU KICK OFF THE CAROL SINGING?
HOW?! WE DON'T HAVE A WORKING SOUND SYSTEM!
DON'T WORRY, VERONICA! I HAVE IT UNDER CONTROL!
DECK THE HALLS WITH BOUGHS OF HOLLY...
FA-LA-LA-LA-LA! LA-LA-LA-LA!!
K
SAY! THIS ISN'T GOING TOO BADLY!
WE'LL HAVE OUR WHITE ELEPHANT GIFT EXCHANGE AFTER THE CAROLLING!
JINGLE BELLS, JINGLE BELLS, JINGLE ALL THE WAY...
K
4

AND SO...
FOR THE LAST SONG OF THE NIGHT WE'LL SING "WHITE CHRISTMAS" WHILE WE LIGHT EACH OTHER'S CANDLES BACK UP!
WHAT A FUN IDEA!
SOON...
LOOK! THE POWER'S BACK ON!
SO IT IS!!
ARE YOU GOING TO FLIP THE SWITCH AND PUT YOUR DISPLAY BACK ON?
I DON'T KNOW IF IT'S SAFE! BESIDES, I THINK WE MANAGED TO LIGHT UP THE SEASON WITH-OUT ALL THE LIGHTS!
ON
OFF
HOW ABOUT ONE MORE SONG?!
YOU'VE GOT IT!
WE WISH YOU A MERRY CHRISTMAS, WE WISH YOU A MERRY CHRISTMAS!
I THINK WE MIGHT JUST HAVE DISCOVERED A NEW HOLIDAY TRADITION!
WELL SAID, VERONICA!
THE END

WORLD OF ARCHIE

Archie in The Snowboard of Education!

THE RIVERDALE SKI CENTER...
ARE YOU SURE THIS IS A GOOD IDEA, ARCHIE?
BETTY IS RIGHT, ARCH.! SNOW-BOARDING CAN BE A LITTLE BIT DANGEROUS FOR SOME PEOPLE...
I DON'T KNOW WHAT ALL THE FUSS IS ABOUT, YOU GUYS.! STOP WORRYING!
YEAH! ONCE CAPTAIN KLUTZOID HERE DECIDES TO BREAK EVERY BONE IN HIS BODY, JUST STAND CLEAR.! HE'LL NEVER LEARN! HA!
REGGIE!
STAFF
JEFF SHULTZ PENCILS
JIM AMASH INKS
GLENN WHITMORE COLORS
JACK MORELLI LETTERS & STORY

YOU'RE REALLY NOT JOINING US, RON?
NO, THIS LODGE STAYS IN THE LODGE! I'LL BE SITTING BY THE FIRE LETTING PEOPLE ADMIRE MY NEW OSCAR DeLAURENTIS SNOWSUIT!
IT'S MY GIFT.
WHOA!
SPROING
PLOOF
SWAKK
YEOWTCH!
YOU'RE OFF TO A FLYING START, PAL O' MINE!
ARE YOU OKAY, ARCH?
YEAH, BETTY... BUT THEY OUGHT TO SALT THOSE STEPS!
HA!
HE'LL NEVER LEARN!
SOON, ON THE CHAIR LIFT...
JUST BE CAREFUL, ARCH!
STOP WORRYING, JUGHEAD!
I DON'T GET WHY EVERYONE THINKS I'M SO CLUMSY!
IT'S A REAL PUZZLER...
2

AT THE TOP...
ACK!
uh--
PLOOF
SPROING
--OH!
HA!
WAKK
YOU'LL NEVER LEARN!
ON THE SLOPES...
HEE! HEE!
SNOOF
KLIK KLIK
WHOOOSH
MUNCH MUNCH
SWOOSH
3

THAT'S SOME GNARLY STEEZ, DUDE!
WATCH OUT! YOU'RE GONNA HIT THAT BOOTER, BRO!
Whoa! WHAT?! WHOA!
YEEOWW!!
SPROING
oh, NO.
WAK
MAN! THAT WAS ONE RAD WRECK, DUDE!
YOU'D BETTER STICK TO THE GREENIES 'TIL YOU LEARN TO SHRED, BRO!
UGH! THAT'S ENOUGH FOR ONE DAY. I'M SURE THE GANG IS AT THE BOTTOM ALREADY!
4

BACK AT THE LODGE...
HA! CHECK OUT OL' CRASH ANDREWS! YOU WERE GOING UP AND DOWN LIKE A BUSTED WINDOW SHADE OUT THERE, BUDDY!
YOU'LL NEVER LEARN.!!
CUT IT OUT, REGGIE! I SAY HE GETS AN "A" FOR EFFORT.!
LOOK OUT, ARCH! YOUR BOARD IS CAUGHT ON THE DOOR JAMB!
SPROING
HARDEE HAR--
SMAK
THE DAY'S NOT A TOTAL LOSS, ARCH! AT LEAST YOU LEARNED HOW TO DUCK!
AND MAYBE--JUST MAYBE--MANTLE GOT A LITTLE EDUCATION, TOO!
END

HEY, LOOK! POP'S IS HAVING A COMPETITIVE EATING CONTEST!
EVERYONE KNOWS THAT JUGHEAD IS A "STOMACH"-IN FOR THAT!
MEGA BURGER EATING CONTEST
I'M NOT SO SURE! THERE'S GOT TO BE OTHER COMPETITIVE EATERS IN TOWN!
GRANTED-- BUT YOU'RE THE ROCK STAR!
Archie IN BURGER BONANZA!
BILL GOLLIHER STORY
JEFF SHULTZ PENCILS
JIM AMASH INKS
WHITMORE-COLORS MORELLI-LETTERS
JUGHEAD! ARE YOU HERE TO SIGN UP FOR THE NEW MEGA BURGER EATING CONTEST?
SEE, PAL! YOUR LEGEND PRECEDES YOU!
TRY THE NEW LOADED MEGA
SIGN
1

THANKS FOR SIGNING UP! IT WILL BE AN HONOR TO HAVE YOU PARTICIPATE! SEE YOU ON THE BIG DAY!
I JUST HOPE I DON'T LET MY PUBLIC DOWN!
SIGN UP
IMA HOGG
GHANNA BARPH
JUGHEAD JONES
NEXT DAY...
POP IS TEXTING ME! HE WANTS ME TO COME RIGHT OVER! LET'S GO!
BONK
DING
SOON...
JUGHEAD, IT SEEMS THAT YOUR FELLOW COMPETITORS HAVE A PROBLEM WITH YOU!
WHAT DO YOU MEAN?
THE OTHERS WHO SIGNED UP REFUSE TO COMPETE WITH YOU ON A LEVEL PLAYING FIELD!
WHAT?!
WHY, THAT'S UN-AMERICAN!
WE SEE YOU AS A LOCAL STAR WHO CAN'T BE BEAT!
DOES THAT MEAN I GET THE PRIZE WITHOUT THE CHANCE TO EAT ALL THOSE BURGERS?
NOT EXACTLY! I PROPOSE WE SET UP A HANDICAP!
Whoa! TAKE IT EASY, POP! PUT DOWN THAT SPATULA!
2

NO, AS THE HANDICAPPER, I SAY HOW MANY BURGERS JUGHEAD HAS TO EAT BEFORE EVERY-ONE ELSE GETS STARTED!
OH! LIKE IN GOLF OR OTHER SPORTS WHEN SOMEONE HAS AN UNFAIR ADVANTAGE!

EXACTLY! THAT'S WHY JUGGIE MUST POLISH OFF FIVE LOADED MEGA BURGERS BEFORE THE CONTEST BEGINS!
OKAY... I'LL DO WHAT I HAVE TO DO!

CONTEST DAY!
HERE WE ARE AT OUR FIRST MEGA BURGER EATING COMPETITION!
OUR FAVORED CONTESTANT, JUGHEAD JONES, HAS FOLLOWED THE RULES IMPOSED ON HIM BY DOWNING FIVE BURGERS ALREADY!
BURP! SORRY, JUST MAKING ROOM!
GROSS!

EVERYONE IS ON EQUAL GROUND! LET THE COMPETITION BEGIN!!
ONE!

TWO!
3

THREE!
I-I'M OUT!
FOUR!
SLURP!
I'M DONE FOR!

FIVE!
THAT'S IT! I'M ALL DONE!

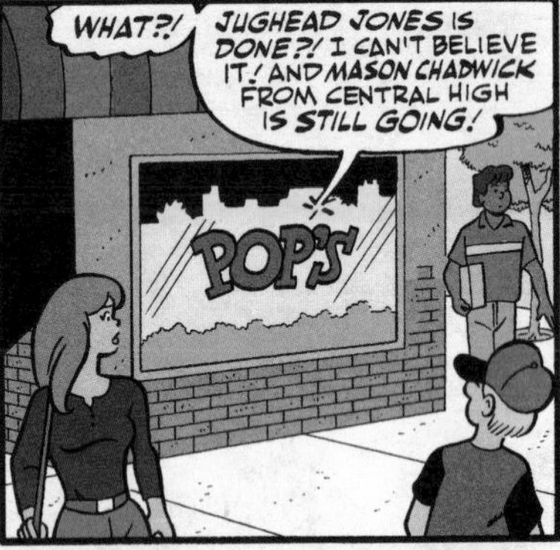
WHAT?!
JUGHEAD JONES IS DONE?! I CAN'T BELIEVE IT! AND MASON CHADWICK FROM CENTRAL HIGH IS STILL GOING!
POP'S

SIX!
MASON, CARE TO GO FOR SEVEN?!
ULP!
4

NO! THAT'S IT!! I NEED TO BE EXCUSED! PRONTO!
DON'T YOU WANT TO CLAIM YOUR PRIZE FIRST?! ONE MEGA BURGER A WEEK FOR A YEAR!

ACK! NO! I--I NEVER WANT TO SEE ANOTHER MEGA BURGER AGAIN!!
WELL, THAT WAS UNEXPECTED!

JUGHEAD, EVEN THOUGH YOU DIDN'T WIN THE TITLE, YOU ARE WELCOME TO THE PRIZE THAT HE DIDN'T WANT!
SURE! I'LL TAKE IT!
PRIZE

I'M JUST SORRY THAT YOU DIDN'T OFFICIALLY WIN THE CONTEST!
LET'S SEE... I GOT TEN LOADED MEGA BURGERS FOR FREE WHILE HE ONLY ATE SIX...

...AND NOW I ALSO GET A FREE MEGA BURGER A WEEK FOR A YEAR!
BY JOVE! I THINK I AM THE WINNER!
GOOD POINT!
TOUCHÉ!
PRIZE
THE END

YOUR NEW SMART REFRIGERATOR IS IMPRESSIVE, VERONICA!

WELL, DADDYKINS SPARED NO EXPENSE, BETTY! IT'S SO SMART, EINSTEIN WOULD BE JEALOUS!

MAYBE I COULD ASK IT FOR HELP WITH MY HOME-WORK!

ARCHIE, IT'S WHAT'S INSIDE THE REFRIGERATOR THAT I'M MOST INTERESTED IN!

FRANCIS BONNET STORY

The FAB K-BROS! PENCILS

JIM AMASH--INKS

GLENN WHITMORE COLORS

JACK MORELLI LETTERS

Archie in SMARTER THAN A-- REFRIGERATOR

YOUR CHOCOLATE WITH TWO CHERRIES AND YOUR GLASS OF COLA WITH SQUEEZED LEMON IS NOW READY.
WE DIDN'T EVEN PUT AN ORDER IN!
IT'S SMART ENOUGH TO KNOW WHAT YOU WANT BEFORE YOU ASK!
I WONDER IF I CAN PLAY VIDEO GAMES ON THIS THING!
ARCHIE! BE CAREFUL! I DON'T KNOW WHAT THOSE BUTTONS DO!
BING
BEEP
BING
IF YOU DIDN'T LIKE YOUR SODA, YOU COULD'VE POURED IT DOWN THE SINK!
I DIDN'T SPILL IT ON PURPOSE!
OH, NO! WE NEED TO CLEAN THAT MESS UP BEFORE IT CAUSES ANY DAMAGE!
HEY! I'M NOT YOUR NAPKIN!
SORRY, BUT YOUR SHIRT WAS THE CLOSEST THING!
YOU SHOULD USE WATER TO WIPE IT UP OR IT WILL GET STICKY!
YOUR WATER IS NOW READY.
ACK!
I ALREADY TOOK MY SHOWER TODAY!
SPLOOSH
WHAT A WASTE OF PERFECTLY GOOD FOOD!
I DON'T THINK THE REFRIGERATOR IS SUPPOSED TO DO THIS!
WE'D BETTER CHECK THE USER MANUAL!
2

YOUR ICE IS NOW READY.!
I LIKE MY DRINKS AT ROOM TEMPERATURE!
SOMEONE NEEDS TO UNPLUG IT!
THAT'S EASIER SAID THAN DONE!
MAYBE WE SHOULD PUT OUR PING PONG SKILLS TO GOOD USE!
FOLLOW MY LEAD, JUG!
I HOPE YOUR NOT LEADING US TO THE HOSPITAL!
YOU'RE DOING IT, ARCHIE!
WE MIGHT BE ABLE TO PULL THE PLUG ON THIS!
SYSTEM OVERRIDE. NOW TAKING CONTROL OF ALL SMART DEVICES!
I THINK YOU SPOKE TOO SOON!
YOUR DISHES ARE NOW READY.!
I DON'T LIKE HOW THIS DANCE IS GOING.!
YOU'RE THE ONE WHO SAID TO FOLLOW YOUR LEAD.!
3

WHEN I WOKE UP THIS MORNING, I REALLY THOUGHT TODAY WOULD BE A NORMAL DAY!

YOUR OVEN TEMPERATURE IS SET NOW.
LOOKS LIKE THINGS ARE ABOUT TO START HEATING UP!
FWOOSH

YOUR POPCORN IS NOW READY!
SAVED TO EAT ANOTHER DAY!
THANKS FOR KNOCKING SOME SENSE INTO US!
WE DIDN'T WANT YOU TWO TO END UP TOAST!

SPEAKING OF TOAST, I THINK THAT MIGHT BE OUR ANSWER!
HOW COULD ANYONE BUT ME BE THINKING OF FOOD AT A TIME LIKE THIS?

THE BURNT TOAST WILL ABSORB THE SOAPY WATER ON THE FLOOR, ALLOWING US TO LEAP OVER AND UNPLUG THE SMART FRIDGE WITHOUT SLIPPING!
GREAT IDEA, ARCH! I NOMINATE YOU!
I'LL GET THE TOASTER'S ATTENTION!

YAH!
NOW, ARCHIE!!
4

OUCH! I'M GONNA FEEL THIS TOMORROW!

AND THAT'S THE END OF THAT!
ARCHIE! YOU DID IT!
WHAT IN THE WORLD HAPPENED HERE?!

ARCHIE!
WHY DO I HAVE THE FEELING THAT THIS IS SOMEHOW ALL YOUR FAULT?!
I-IT WAS THE FRIDGE, MR. LODGE!

ARE YOU GOING TO TELL ME THAT THIS MESS WAS BECAUSE OF MY NEW SMART REFRIGERATOR?!
IT'S NOT MY FAULT THAT YOUR SMART REFRIGERATOR IS SO DUMB!
END

Archie in DON'T MASK ME WHY!

YODEL AY-HEE HOO!!

HAHA! THE MASKED YODELER! THIS SHOW IS CRAZY!

WHAT SHOULD WE WATCH NEXT?

DAN PARENT STORY & PENCILS

BOB SMITH INKS

GLENN WHITMORE COLORS

JACK MORELLI LETTERS

WE SHOULD CAPITALIZE ON THIS!
HOW?!
WE'RE NOT ON TV!
AND I'M NOT PERFORMING IN A MASK ON STAGE!

WE NEED SOMETHING DIFFERENT!
WE SHOULD COMBINE IT WITH ANOTHER POPULAR GENRE!

I'VE GOT IT!! AND IT'S RIGHT UP YOUR ALLEY, TOO!

WE CAN DO IT AND PUT IT ON MY "ME-TUBE" CHANNEL!
WHAT IS IT?! WHAT IS IT?!

ARE YOU READY FOR...
2

...WELCOME, FOLKS, TO THE MASKED CHEF!
THAT'S RIGHT! THE SHOW THAT COMBINES COOK-ING WITH A SENSE OF MYSTERY!

AND JUST WHO IS BEHIND THE MASK OF MONSIEUR BUBU? YOU'LL HAVE TO WAIT AND SEE!

IT'S OBVIOUSLY ARCHIE! WHO ELSE WOULD IT BE?
WE KNOW THAT-- BUT THE VIEWERS, ALL FIVE OF THEM, DON'T KNOW THAT!

WHAT ARE YOU GOING TO PREPARE, MONSIEUR BUBU?
I'M GOING TO MAKE A CHOCOLATE MOUSSE CAKE!

I'LL JUST GET THE INGREDIENTS...
BONK
3

BOOM
WAK
THOK
WHAT HAPPENED TO THE PICTURE?
I THINK THE BUFFOON KNOCKED OVER THE CAMERA WITH HIS BIG DUCK BILL!
SOON
OKAY! SORRY ABOUT THAT--WE'RE BACK ON THE AIR!
I'VE GOT THE INGREDIENTS HERE TO PUT IN THE BOWL...
ER...YOU'RE MISSING THE BOWL!
I CAN'T HELP IT!
GLOOP
I CAN ONLY SEE STRAIGHT AHEAD!
I CAN'T LOOK DOWN IN THIS GIANT HEAD!
SPLOOT
I'LL HELP YOU...
SLOP
NO! I HAVE TO DO THIS MYSELF!
4

OKAY! I THINK I'VE GOT ALL OF THE INGREDIENTS IN THE BOWL...
uhh... IF YOU SAY SO...
BZZZZZZZ
TURN THAT MIXER OFF!! YOU CAN'T SEE WHAT YOU'RE DOING!
WATCH THE CURTAINS!
FWIIIRLL
BZZROW
ACK!
YOWIE!!
ARCHIE!
TAKE OFF THAT GIANT HEAD!!
JUGHEAD!! YOU REVEALED MY IDENTITY AND RUINED THE MYSTERY!
NOT QUITE!
I THINK WE FIGURED OUT WHO IT WAS PRETTY EARLY ON!
HAHA! HAHA!
HA! HA! HA HA!
END

FRANCIS BONNET STORY
The KENNEDY BROTHERS PENCILS
BOB SMITH INKS
GLENN WHITMORE COLORS
JACK MO! LETTS
I CAN'T BELIEVE YOU RENTED THE ENTIRE WATER PARK JUST FOR US, RONNIE!
VERONICA LODGE DOES NOT WAIT IN LINES!
I'M CHECKING OUT THE WATER SLIDE FIRST!
AND I'M CHECKING OUT THE SNACK STAND FIRST!
Archie IN WATERPARKED!
THIS IS ALMOST BETTER THAN SURFING AT THE BEACH!
IT'S WAY BETTER! NO SHARKS TO WORRY ABOUT!
SNACK LATER, JUG! COME JOIN IN THE FUN!
ARCHIE, SNACKING IS FUN!
ICE CREAM
1

THIS WOULD BE MORE FUN WITH MORE FRIENDS!
WE COULD INVITE ALL OF OUR FRIENDS!
LIFE GUARD

YOU'RE RIGHT, BETTY! I'LL TEXT OUT AN INVITE!
MAYBE YOU SHOULD WAIT UNTIL THE RIDE ENDS!

REGGIE, GINGER, TONI! I'M GLAD YOU WERE ABLE TO COME!
YOU SHOULD'VE INVITED ME FIRST, NOT ARCHIE! I'M MORE FUN!
WRONG AS USUAL, REGGIE!
I HOPE JUGHEAD LEFT SOME FOOD FOR ME IN THOSE SNACK STANDS!
I'M NOT PROMISING ANYTHING, TONI!

I HOPE YOU DON'T MIND, BUT I'VE INVITED A FEW OTHER FRIENDS TO JOIN US!
THE MORE THE MERRIER, GINGER!

DO YOU THINK THESE WILL BE ENOUGH SNACKS FOR US?
PROBABLY... UNTIL WE GET TO THE END OF THIS RIDE.
2

SO, CARROT-TOP... DO YOU WANT TO RACE ME TO THE BOTTOM, OR ARE YOU TOO SCARED?
UH... OF COURSE I'M NOT SCARED!

I HOPE ARCHIE DOESN'T NOTICE MY EYES ARE CLOSED!
I HOPE REG DOESN'T NOTICE THAT MY EYES ARE CLOSED!

I TOTALLY WON THAT!
NO WAY! THAT RACE WAS ALL MINE!
HOW DO EITHER OF YOU KNOW WHO WON?! YOU BOTH HAD YOUR EYES CLOSED!!

ER... HI, MIDGE, MOOSE, AND DILTON! WHEN DID YOU GET HERE?
JUST NOW! ALONG WITH A BUNCH OF OTHER FRIENDS!

STUDYING THE MECHANICS OF THIS WAVE POOL IS FASCINATING!
DILTON, THIS ISN'T A WAVE POOL! THIS IS MOOSE!
UH... SORRY!

YOU TWO WERE AWESOME! IT'LL MAKE GREAT FOOTAGE FOR THE WATER PARK DOCUMENTARY I'M FILMING!
BUT RAJ... NANCY AND I GOT HIT WITH A MOOSE-MADE TIDAL WAVE!
I KNOW, CHUCK! IT'S A COMEDY!
3

I SHOULD GO AND FIND BETTY AND VERONICA!
THE ONLY PERSON YOU NEED TO FIND IS *ME*!
CHERYL?
ARCHIE, *THERE'S* A RIDE WE NEED TO *GO ON TOGETHER*!
WELL...
TUNNEL OF LOVE
I CAN'T *BELIEVE* THAT CHERYL!
DON'T WORRY! THAT RIDE IS ABOUT TO BE *OUT OF ORDER*!
ISN'T IT *ROMANTIC* IN HERE, ARCHIE?
WHAT'S GOING ON?!
I DIDN'T EXPECT THINGS BETWEEN US TO MOVE *THIS* FAST!
SO GLAD YOU WERE ABLE TO JOIN IN ALL THE WATER PARK FUN, CHERYL!
I BELIEVE YOU WERE LOOKING FOR *US*, ARCHIE?
4

SORRY, I GOT... DISTRACTED.
LUCKILY, WE WERE HERE TO DISTRACT YOU FROM YOUR DISTRACTION!

THERE YOU ARE! EVERYONE'S WAITING FOR YOU THREE!
WAITING FOR US? WHAT FOR?!

FOR YOU TO JOIN US AT THE WAVE POOL PARTY!

DO WE STILL HAVE THE PARK TO OUR-SELVES?
OF COURSE, JUG! IT'S JUST US AND A FEW HUNDRED OF OUR CLOSEST FRIENDS!
END

Archie in STUCK ON VR!

THIS NEW *VR HEADSET* YOU GOT IS AMAZING, ARCHIE! I FEEL LIKE I'M IN *ANOTHER WORLD*!

JUGHEAD, THE ONLY THINGS THEY HAVEN'T PERFECTED IN VR ARE *TASTE* AND *SMELL*!

LODGE INDUSTRIES VR SET

FRANCIS BONNET STORY

JEFF SHULTZ PENCILS

JIM AMASH INKS

GLENN WHITMORE COLORS

JACK MORELLI LETTERS

MAYBE MR. LODGE KNOWS HOW TO TAKE THIS THING OFF!
AND IT'S A GOOD EXCUSE TO SEE VERONICA! I'LL DRIVE YOU!
ARE WE THERE YET?
WE WOULD BE IF YOU'D STOP COMPLAINING!
I'M GETTING SHOCKS FROM THE VR HEADSET! I DON'T THINK IT'S COMPATIBLE WITH YOUR CAR!
YIKES! WE NEED ANOTHER WAY TO GET YOU THERE!
THIS WILL GET YOU TO MR. LODGE WITH ZERO SHOCKS!
AND I'LL TURN ON THE VR SKATEBOARD GAME TO MAKE THIS RIDE A LITTLE MORE ENJOYABLE!
I'M ABOUT TO BEAT MY HIGH SCORE! HOW ARE THINGS LOOKING IN THE REAL WORLD, ARCHIE?
2

GNARLY! IF ONLY YOU COULD WALK AS WELL AS YOU SKATE, JUG!

WHA! I JUST GOT FAST-TRACKED!
STEP ON YOUR VIRTUAL BRAKES!

HEY!
BONK
LOOK OUT!!
NEW HIGH SCORE! I WISH EVERYONE COULD SEE HOW GREAT I'M DOING!

WHERE ARE YOU GOING, JUG?! I CAN'T CATCH WHAT I CAN'T SEE!!
ZOOM

H-HE'S GONE! HOW COULD I LOSE HIM? IT'S NOT LIKE HE'S A SET OF KEYS!
3

I SAW HIM SKATE INTO THE CHOCK'LIT SHOPPE!
THANKS, TONI! BUT HOW DID HE FIND IT?! HE CAN'T SEE!!

I'M SURE HE FOLLOWED THE SMELL OF FOOD! IT'S WHAT I WOULD'VE DONE!

JUGHEAD!! I THOUGHT I'D LOST YOU!
WHEN IN DOUBT, YOU CAN ALWAYS FIND ME IN A PLACE WHERE FOOD IS SERVED!

I ONLY WISH THE REAL WORLD HAD BURGERS LIKE THIS!

I THOUGHT YOU WANTED TO GET THAT VR HEAD-SET OFF!
BUT I'M STILL HUNGRY!

THIS TIME I'LL STEER YOU THE WHOLE WAY SO THERE ARE NO ACCIDENTS!
LEAD THE WAY, ARCH!
4

ARCHIE!
WHAT AN UNEXPECTED SURPRISE!
HI, VERONICA! I WAS HOPING TO SEE YOUR DAD! THIS VR HEADSET HE MADE IS FAULTY...

FAULTY?!
NOTHING LODGE INDUSTRIES MAKES IS FAULTY!!

THERE'S A REMOVE BUTTON CLEARLY LABELED RIGHT HERE!
Oh... uh... I MUST HAVE MISSED THAT...

OOPS!
!

BOOF
BANG
KRAK

MY COMPANY MADE THAT VR HEADSET FOOL-PROOF... BUT WE SHOULD'VE MADE IT
ARCHIE-PROOF!!
END

ANOTHER YEAR, ANOTHER FRESH START! WHAT COULD BE BETTER?
STILL SLEEPING IN FOR ONE THING! yawn!
RIVERDALE HIGH est. 1941
WHAT FUN IS THAT? YOU WOULDN'T GET THE CHANCE TO WELCOME ME BACK!
NO!
IT--IT CAN'T BE--!
TRULA TWYST!
in
JUGHEAD'S GREATEST NEMESIS!
BUT YOU MOVED TO EUROPE FOR YOUR MOM'S JOB!
SO I DID! BUT SHE TRANSFERRED BACK THIS YEAR-- SO HERE I AM!!
BILL GOLLIHER STORY & PENCILS
JIM AMASH INKS
GLENN WHITMORE COLORS
JACK MORELLI LETTERS
1

NOW WHERE'S THE CROWNED ONE? I'VE MISSED MY VICTIM... ER... FRIEND!
HAVEN'T SEEN HIM YET! LOOK AT THE TIME! BETTER GET TO CLASS!
WE CAN'T LET HER RUIN THE START OF JUGHEAD'S SCHOOL YEAR! WE MUST KEEP THEM APART!
UH-OH! HERE HE COMES NOW!
QUICK, JUGGIE! IN HERE!
THE BROOM CLOSET?! WHAT'S UP?
UH... PRINCIPAL WEATHERBEE IS OUT TO BAN EAR-BUDS AND WE'RE PROTECTING YOUR RIGHTS!
PSST! TRULA TWYST IS BACK AND WE'RE TRYING TO KEEP JUG FROM FINDING OUT!
GOOD IDEA! THAT COULD SEND HIM OFF THE DEEP END!
BROOM CLOSET
HI, BOYS! YOURS TRULA IS BACK FROM EUROPE!
YOU'VE GOT TO TELL US ALL ABOUT IT! DON'T LEAVE OUT ANY DETAILS!
PSST! SHE'S HERE! LET'S MOVE HIM!
OKAY, JUG! WE'RE GOING, SO I'M COVERING YOUR BUDS!
2

THE LOUVRE WAS FABU-LOUS!
LET'S GET HIM TO THE CAFETERIA!
BRILLIANT! NO ONE HAS A CLUE THAT I'M LISTENING TO MY MUSIC!
WHY IS HE HERE? IT'S THE FIRST DAY OF SCHOOL! I'M NOT THAT WELL-STOCKED!
THE BEE'S BANNING EAR BUDS --
--SO THEY'RE PROTECTING ME!
HE'S NOT ALLOWED IN HERE, EITHER!
BONK
UH... SHE'S RIGHT! LET'S GET OUT OF HERE!
MS. BEAZLEY, HAVE YOU SEEN JUGHEAD?
YES! I JUST KICKED HIM OUT--ALONG WITH BETTY AND VERONICA!
THAT WAS CLOSE! LET'S GET TO THE GYM!
YEAH! THAT'S PROBABLY A GOOD CHOICE!
I APPRECIATE YOU GIRLS WORKING SO HARD TO PROTECT MY MUSICAL LIBERTIES!
GYMNASIUM
3

THE LOCKER ROOMS! WE SHOULD BE SAFE THERE!
BUT GIRLS' OR GUYS'? WHICH WOULD YOU-KNOW-WHO PICK?
LOCKER ROOMS

SHE'S A FEMALE! I SAY WE HIT THE GUYS' LOCKERS!
LUCKILY, THERE'S NO FIRST PERIOD P.E. CLASSES!

MEAN-WHILE...
DO TELL US MORE ABOUT YOUR EURO-PEAN ADVENTURES, TRULA!
YOU CAN'T FOOL MY PSYCHOLOGICAL MIND! YOU'RE DISTRACTING ME TO KEEP ME AWAY FROM JUGHEAD!

IF BETTY AND VERONICA ARE HIDING HIM, I'M SURE THIS IS THE LAST PLACE THEY THINK I'D LOOK!
LOCKER ROOMS
NOW WOULD IT BE THE GIRLS' OR THE GUYS' LOCKER ROOMS?
HMMMM...

THEY WOULD THINK I'D LOOK IN THE GIRLS' LOCKER ROOM FIRST, SO THEY MUST BE HIDING IN THE GUYS'!
4

...AND STAY OUT!
HOW WERE WE SUPPOSED TO KNOW YOU WERE IN THERE, COACH?!
AH-HAH! FINALLY WE MEET AGAIN FACE-TO-FACE!
THAT'S EXACTLY WHAT WE WERE TRYING TO AVOID WITH THIS EAR BUD COVER-UP!!
SO THE BEE'S NOT BANNING EARBUDS?!
NO! WE JUST SAID THAT TO PROTECT YOU FROM HER!
HE'S JUST PUTTING HIS BUDS BACK IN!
WHAT?! AREN'T YOU EVEN GOING TO LET ME TELL YOU "HELLO," JUGHEAD JONES?!
OH, SURE! RIGHT AFTER I GET DONE LISTENING TO THIS NEW PLAYLIST OF THE OTHER TOP ANNOYING SOUNDS ON EARTH!
WOW! HE TOOK THAT WELL!
TRULA, IT SEEMS YOUR SPELL HAS BEEN BROKEN!
WE'LL SEE ABOUT THAT!
MMMMM
THE END

SLAM
SO THE GIRLS DON'T LIKE MY GIFTS--I'LL FIND SOMEONE WHO DOES!
BOO-OOGA BOO-OOGA
WHAT THE HECK?!
DON'T FEAR, MORTAL! YOUR FRIENDS ARE HERE FOR THIS HALLOWEEN PARTY TO DIE FOR!
BOO-BUS
ISN'T THE BOO-BUS COOL?!
IT'S A MOBILE DJ BOOTH WE RENTED TO MAKE THIS PARTY ROCK!
NICE COSTUME, FRANKEN-ARCH!
THANKS! NOT BAD YOURSELF, DRAC-HEAD!
BOO-BUS
Archie IN
HALLOWEEN HULLABALOO!
BILL GOLLIHER STORY & PENCILS
JIM AMASH INKS
JACK MORELLI LETTERS
GLENN WHITMORE COLORS
1

THANKS! I DO LIKE MY BURGERS RARE WITH A LOT OF KETCHUP!
HEY! THAT'S A COOL NECKLACE! MIND IF I WEAR IT WITH MY COSTUME?
SURE! THE GIRLS DIDN'T WANT THEM! THEY GOT ALL WEIRD! I'LL SLIP THE BRACELET ON FOR NOW!
EVERYONE IS ARRIVING--LET'S GET THIS PARTY STARTED!
AND SO...
I'LL KICK OFF THE MUSIC AND LIGHT SHOW!
BOO-BUS
AWESOME!
THE PARTY'S UNDERWAY! IT WILL TAKE OUR MIND OFF THE CURSED JEWELRY!
Shh! DON'T EVEN SPEAK OF IT!
WE DIDN'T MEAN TO BE RUDE--BUT THAT JEWELRY IS CURSED!
CURSED?! YOU GUYS ARE REALLY BUYING INTO THIS HALLOWEEN THEME! THAT'S RIDICULOUS!
THAT'S WHAT WE THOUGHT AT FIRST!
LET'S DANCE TO GET YOUR MINDS OFF OF IT!
2

WE'VE GOT GREAT MUSIC, LIGHTS AND FOG THANKS TO THE BOO-BUS!
JUST FORGET ABOUT THIS SILLY BRACELET AND NECK-LACE!
EEK!
Y-YOU'RE WEARING IT!!
BOO-B

SABRINA, DID I MENTION I'M DEEJAYING THIS EVENT WITH THE BOO-BUS HERE?
UH, REGGIE! YOU JUST STARTED IT ROLLING!
CREEEK

OH, NO! I DIDN'T SET THE BRAKE!
IT'S HEADED FOR THE REFRESHMENT TABLE!
!
BOO-BUS

JUGHEAD! GET OUT OF THE WAY!!
BUT SOMEONE HAS TO SAVE THE FOOD!
BOO

I'LL ZAP JUG TO SAFETY IN THE POOL!
WHOA! WHAT'S HAPPENING?!
KRASH
ZAP
SPLOOSH
3

JUGHEAD AND THE FOOD JUST FLEW INTO THE POOL! PUNCHBOWL AND ALL!
OH, NO! IS HE OKAY?!
THE WATER IS CHURNING AND TURNING... RED!
IS IT THE FOOD COLORING FROM THE PUNCH... OR SOMETHING ELSE?!
SCREECH!
WHO DARES TRY TO DESTROY DRAC-HEAD AND HIS SNACKS?!
LOOK! IT'S THE NECKLACE'S FAULT!
HAHA! HA! HA!
SPLASH

SEE? EVERYTHING IS FINE! I'M GOING TO MOVE THE BOO-BUS BACK!
CAREFUL! THE GROUND IS ALL WET FROM THE BIG SPLASH!

NOT TO MENTION THAT STRING OF LIGHTS-- YOU MAY GET A SHOCK!
GYAH!!
BZAT
4

IT SET OFF A CHAIN REACTION!
THE LIGHTS ARE ALL BLOWING OUT!
BOOM BANG
SHANG-A-LANG

WHOO! WHOO!
KRACKLE
NOW THERE ARE WEIRD SOUNDS COMING FROM THE BOO-BUS!
THIS IS TOO SPOOKY! EVERYONE OUT! PARTY'S OVER!

LOOK! AN OWL FLEW IN AND PERCHED ON THE MICROPHONE! THAT'S THE CULPRIT! IT'S ALL NOTHING!
WHOO!
NO! IT'S THE JEWELRY!! IT'S CURSED! WE HAVE TO GET RID OF IT-- ONCE AND FOR ALL!

DON'T WORRY! JUGHEAD AND I WILL TAKE CARE OF IT ON THE WAY HOME!
MAKE SURE THAT IT'S GONE-- PERMANENTLY!!

AND SO...
ALRIGHT! THE NECKLACE IS THROWN AWAY! NOW FOR THE BRACELET!
WAIT! THIS IS SILLY! I THINK JELLYBEAN MIGHT LIKE THIS!
TRASH

FINE-- JUST DON'T TELL THE GIRLS THAT YOU KEPT IT!
BESIDES, WHAT HARM CAN A LITTLE JEWELRY DO?
TRASH
BZZZTT
The END?!

Archie IN O Christmas Tree
WOW!
THE CHRISTMAS TREE LOOKS GREAT!
IT SHOULD! I SPENT ALL DAY DECORATING IT!
DAN PARENT STORY & PENCILS
BOB SMITH INKS
GLENN WHITMORE COLORS
JACK MORELLI LETTERS
YOUR DAD AND I ARE LEAVING NOW TO VISIT AUNT LOUISE FOR A FEW DAYS!
HAVE FUN!
REMEMBER TO WATER THE TREE, ARCHIE!
I WILL!
1

SEE THAT YOU DO!
YOU CAN COUNT ON ME!

A FEW DAYS LATER...
THIS MARATHON OF "THE DEAD AMONG US" WAS AWESOME!

ALTHOUGH IT DID TAKE QUITE A WHILE TO WATCH ALL OF THE EPISODES!
SLURP

WHAT'S UP, VEGAS?
WHY THE WATERING CAN?

OHMIGOSH!! I FORGOT TO WATER THE TREE!
I'D BETTER GET ON IT!
AH-AH-AH-- CHOO!
2

FWUMP
!
OOO
OOO
TINKLE
TINKLE
TINKLE
TINKLE
Oh, NO! THE TREE'S BEEN REDUCED TO A PILE OF DRY NEEDLES!
I'M DOOMED!!
I'D BETTER GET A NEW TREE, PRONTO!
BUT...
NOT A TREE TO BE FOUND ANYWHERE!
HEY!!
I THINK WE HAVE AN ARTIFICIAL TREE UP IN THE ATTIC!
YIKES! ALL WE HAVE IS THIS OLD SILVER TREE!
Hmm! MAYBE IF I COVER IT WITH A TON OF ORNAMENTS, NO ONE WILL NOTICE! IT'S WORTH A SHOT!
3

SO...
WELL, WHAT DO YOU THINK?
IS THERE A TREE IN THERE SOME-WHERE?!

VERY FUNNY! WHAT CHOICE DO I HAVE?
TO TELL THE TRUTH!

NOT AN OPTION!!
WELL, I TRIED!
AND...
WE'RE HOME! HAPPY CHRISTMAS EVE!
ULP!!

HELLO, DEAR! WE-- OH, MY! WHAT HAPPENED TO THE TREE?!
I ADDED A FEW MORE DECORATIONS!

DON'T YOU LIKE IT?
OH... UH... OF COURSE I DO! IT'S SO... SO... FESTIVE!
4

WELL, WE'RE TIRED FROM TRAVELING!
WE'LL SEE YOU BRIGHT AND EARLY!

SEE YOU IN THE MORNING!
Phew! SO FAR, SO GOOD!

CHRISTMAS MORNING...
WHAT ARE YOU DOING, MARY?
JUST CLEARING OFF SOME OF THESE DECORATIONS!

I WANT TO SEE SOME OF OUR BEAUTIFUL TREE AFTER ALL!
ULP! NOW I'M DOOMED!

I CAN EXPLAIN!!
EXPLAIN? EXPLAIN WHAT, ARCHIE?

Huh?!
THE TREE! HOW?! WHAT?!
Merry Christmas, ARCHIE!
END

RIVERDALE SANTA CON

I *LOVE* THE CHRISTMAS DAY **SANTA CON!**

EVERYONE IS SO *FESTIVE*, ARCHIE!

RON ROBBINS STORY

The FAB k-BROS! PENCILS

JIM AMASH INKS

GLENN WHITMORE COLORS

JACK MORELLI LETTERS

Archie SANTA CON CARNE

SANTA! IS IT REALLY YOU?!
AND WHY THE LONG FACE? IT'S CHRISTMAS!

HI, KIDS! I DECIDED TO PICK UP A SACK FULL OF BURGERS FOR THE ELVES AND SOME FLOWERS FOR MRS. CLAUS BEFORE HEADING HOME!

I LEFT THE BURGERS FROM POP'S IN THE SLEIGH, AND WENT OVER TO FELICIA'S FLORALS FOR THIS BEAUTIFUL BOUQUET! BUT WHEN I CAME BACK, THE SLEIGH WAS GONE!!

DID YOU SAY GULP! A SACK OF BURGERS?
JUGHEAD!!
2

EARLIER THAT MORNING!
C'MON, HOT DOG! TWO OF POP'S CHILI BURGERS WILL REALLY HIT THE SPOT!
GRUMBLE
POP

SORRY, JUGHEAD!
THE KITCHEN IS SUPER BACKED-UP AFTER A VERY LARGE ORDER FROM KRIS KRINGLE!

3

POP'S

4

NORTH
POLE
TOY FACTORY
HIRING ELVES
?
?
CLAUS
ELF P.D.
THE END

WELCOME TO: MIDVILLE™

STARRING: THAT WILKIN BOY!

OHMIGOSH! I CAN'T BELIEVE SHE WAS THE KILLER!

I KNEW IT! DIDN'T I TELL YOU?!

DAN PARENT STORY & PENCILS

BOB SMITH INKS | GLENN WHITMORE COLORS | JACK MORELLI LETTERS

AND KJ APA!
AND CAMILA MENDES...
...OR LILI REINHART...
...BUT THEN AGAIN THERE'S MADELAINE PETSCH!
OKAY! YOU'VE MADE YOUR POINT, BINGO!
AND ON THAT NOTE, I'VE GOT TO GO!
NONE OF THOSE GIRLS CAN HOLD A CANDLE TO YOU, SAMANTHA!
NICE SAVE!
≈YAWN!≈ I'D BETTER HIT THE HAY!
ALL THAT BINGE WATCHING CAN WEAR A GUY OUT!
Hmm... I WONDER WHAT A SHOW BASED ON MY LIFE HERE IN MIDVILLE WOULD BE LIKE... Zzzz...
2

MIDVILLE™
STARRING:
ZAC EFRON AS BINGO WILKIN
APPROPRIATE CASTING FOR SURE!
SCARLETT JOHANSSON AS SAMANTHA SMYTHE
I CAN SEE IT!
BRAD PITT AS SAMPSON SMYTHE
NOW THAT'S A STRETCH!
GEORGE CLOONEY AS UNCLE HERMAN
WOW! UNCLE HERMAN SHOULD BE VERY GRATEFUL!
TIMOTHÉE CHALAMET AS TEDDY
THIS IS GETTING ABSURD!

BINGO! WHAT'S WRONG?
IT'S MR. SMYTHE! HE'S ALWAYS ON MY BACK!

I'VE HAD IT WITH HIM!
OHMIGOSH! HAVE YOU HEARD THE NEWS?!

MR. SMYTHE IS DEAD!
AND THEY SUSPECT FOUL PLAY!
?!
HEY! DON'T LOOK AT ME!!
A LOT OF PEOPLE COULD HAVE DONE THIS!

SO...
Oh, DADDY! WHO DID THIS TO YOU?!?
WELL, THERE'S NOTHING WE CAN DO NOW... SO--

--LET'S GO TO THE BEACH!
BINGO! HOW CAN YOU BE SO COLD?! MY DADDY IS GONE! :SOB!:
YEAH, BINGO!
4

WHAT'S WRONG WITH YOU?! LET ME HOLD YOU, SAMANTHA!
LEAVE HER ALONE, TEDDY!
MAKE ME!
ALL RIGHT! I WILL!!
POW
BOP
WOK

THOK
BUMP
MR. SMYTHE! YOU'RE ALIVE!
THAT'S RIGHT! I FAKED MY DEATH TO SEE HOW YOU FOOLS WOULD TREAT SAMANTHA!
LET'S JUST SAY YOU BOTH FAILED THE TEST

NOW I'M GONNA LET YOU HAVE IT!!
FEET DON'T FAIL ME NOW!

BINGO! WAKE UP!
HE'S SLEEP-WALKING! OR RATHER SLEEP-RUNNING!
THAT'S IT! NO MORE WATCHING "RIVERDALE" BEFORE BED!
The END

WORLD OF B&V

Betty and Veronica in The CHALLENGE
JAMIE ROTANTE WRITER
BILL GALVAN PENCILS
BEN GALVAN INKS
GLENN WHITMORE COLORS
JACK MORELLI LETTERS
...THIS HAS OVER 10,000 VIEWS?
1

FRIES
TUNA MELT
WHY ARE YOU SO SURPRISED, JUGHEAD?
BECAUSE IT'S JUST YOU AND BETTY DOING DANCES.
IT'S NOT JUST DANCING-- WE ALSO HAVE INFORMATIVE VIDEOS ON CURRENT ISSUES.
...AND MEMES!
I LOVE THOSE ME-ME THINGS, THEY'RE HILARIOUS!
I JUST DON'T GET YOU KIDS NOWADAYS AND YOUR "MODERN TECHNOLOGY"--
BOINK
OOh! A COSMO GO HOTSPOT IS IN THE PARKING LOT! GOTTA GO!
2

Oh, WHO CARES WHAT HE THINKS--YOU LIKE OUR VIDEOS, RIGHT, ARCHIEKINS?
S-SURE, VERONICA...
EVEN IF YOU SPEND SO MUCH TIME ON THEM WE NEVER GO ON DATES ANYMORE...
OHMYGOSH!
BTX IS HOSTING A CHALLENGE--!
WHOEVER HAS THE MOST CREATIVE VIDEO ON FLIPFLOP WINS A GRAND PRIZE...
BTX WILL PLAY IN OUR HOMETOWN?!
BTX?!
POP'S
3

WHERE DID THEY ALL RUSH OFF TO?
I DON'T KNOW! VERONICA MENTIONED BTX AND FLIPFLOP--
--AND THEY ALL TOOK OFF RUNNING!

DID YOU SAY BTX?!

WHAT'S BTX? IS THAT LIKE A BLT?
NO, THEY'RE THIS POP GROUP EVERYONE LOVES. LOOKS LIKE THEY'RE HOSTING SOME KIND OF VIDEO CHALLENGE...
CHALLENGE, Eh?

SOON...
REGGIE! GET OUT OF HERE! WE FINALLY PERFECTED THAT MOVE!
RIVERDALE HIGH SCHOOL est. 1941
YOUR DANCE VIDEOS ARE GOOD--BUT YOU CAN'T EXPECT TO WIN THIS BTX CHALLENGE DOING THE SAME STUFF AS EVERYONE ELSE.
YOU NEED TO GET INVENTIVE.
DANCE FRIDAY!
AND WHY SHOULD WE LISTEN TO YOU?
BECAUSE WHO KNOWS MORE ABOUT WINNING THAN ME?
JUST LOOK AT MY FLIPFLOP--
WAIT--YOU'RE FLIPMONSTER23?!
THAT'S ONE OF THE MOST POPULAR FLIPFLOP ACCOUNTS EVER!
THE ONE AND ONLY.
NOW, IF YOU LISTEN TO ME, I PROMISE YOU'LL WIN THIS CHALLENGE.
BUT WE'LL NEED TO FILM A FEW PRACTICE VIDEOS FIRST...
5

LOOKING GOOD, LADIES!

AAAHHHH!!

WHY ARE WE BEING DRAGGED INTO THIS, REGGIE?
THE MORE PEOPLE INVOLVED, THE BETTER.
R
S

Hmmm... I GUESS THAT WORKS...

NOW THAT'S MORE LIKE IT...BUT STILL, WE NEED SOMETHING BETTER...SOMETHING BIGGER!
WOK

MEAN-
WHILE,
ON
BTX's
TOUR
BUS...

BOYS, I THINK WE FOUND OURSELVES A WINNER... CHECK IT OUT.

WOW-- THOSE GIRLS CAN DANCE!
YEAH, THEY DEFINITELY EARNED IT.
SO, WHERE ARE WE HEADED TO PERFORM?

RIVERDALE, USA!
RIVERDALE-- WHERE'S THAT?
Oh, IT'S IN--
GOOD MORNING, RIVERDALE!
7

THANK YOU ALL FOR COMING HERE BRIGHT AND EARLY. I PROMISE YOU THIS WILL WIN THE BTX CHALLENGE!

REGGIE! YOU'VE BEEN FILMING ALL OF OUR MOST EMBARRASSING MOMENTS AND PUTTING THEM UP ON FLIPFLOP?!
I THOUGHT YOU WANTED TO WIN, VERONICA.

HOW IS THIS WINNING?! WE LOOK LIKE FOOLS!
AND YOU'RE NOT FLIPMONSTER23 AT ALL, ARE YOU?!

OF COURSE NOT. LIKE I'D ACTUALLY HIDE MY FACE FROM THE PUBLIC?
BUT TRUST ME ON THIS ONE-- THIS VIDEO WILL CLINCH IT FOR US.

WHY WOULD WE EVER TRUST YOU AGAIN?
AND WHAT IS THIS, EXACTLY?

THE MINTOZ AND SODA CHALLENGE! DILTON, TAKE IT AWAY.
THE GIANT VAT IS FILLED HALFWAY WITH A FEW GALLONS OF ORANGE SODA.
SOON, EVERYONE IN TOWN WILL DROP IN THEIR OPEN PACKS OF MINTOZ CANDY AND IT WILL CREATE A STELLAR SURPRISE!

IS IT DANGER-OUS?
OF COURSE NOT. SEE, WE'RE GOING FOR THE LONGEST ONGOING STREAM, NOT LARGEST BY VOLUME.
AS LONG AS WE HANDLE IT CAREFULLY AND NOT HAVE EVERYONE DO IT AT THE SAME TIME, WE CAN CONTROL THE--
8

OKAY, EVERYONE-- FIRE AWAY!
FSSSSSS
REGGIE-- NOOO!
FWOOM

WHAT A CUTE LITTLE TOWN. I'LL BET THEY'VE NEVER HAD SOMETHING THIS BIG HAPPEN HERE!
WELCOME TO Riverdale The TOWN WITH PEP!
REGGIE!!
Uh-OH...
HEY, WAITAMINUTE-- LOOK!
WOW! WE WEREN'T EXPECTING THIS KIND OF A WELCOME! IF YOU DON'T MIND US, WE'LL JUST PERFORM OUR SONGS UP HERE!
IF BETTY AND VERONICA ARE HERE, WE WOULD LOVE TO HAVE THEM JOIN US!
WE DID IT!!
AND I HELPED!
NOW, THIS IS A FLIPFLOP VIDEO WORTHY OF 10,000 VIEWS...
The END

Betty and Veronica in Romancing PETER PAN

WELL, WELL! IF IT ISN'T PETER PAN! WHATEVER BRINGS YOU TO LONDON? YOUR SHADOW IS STILL ATTACHED!

VENDY--IT'S BINKERBELL! SHE'S STILL EXTREMELY JEALOUS OF OUR RELATION-SHIP!

SHE'S WREAKING HAVOC IN NEVER-LAND!

BILL GOLLIHER STORY

DAN PARENT PENCILS

BOB SMITH INKS

GLENN WHITMORE COLORS

JACK MORELLI LETTERS

I HAVE MAGIC ON MY SIDE!
AND I HAVE SIZE! LET'S GO AT IT!

GIRLS! THIS IS NO SOLUTION! LET ME TAKE BINKERBELL BACK TO NEVERLAND TO COOL OFF!
LET'S GO!
GOOD RIDDANCE!

Hmmm... I MIGHT NOT BE ABLE TO GET VENDY OUT OF THE PICTURE... BUT I KNOW WHO CAN!
AND SO...

BINKERBELL! WHAT BRINGS YOU HERE TO SEE THE ONE AND ONLY--
--CAPTAIN SNOOK?
WE HAVE A COMMON PROBLEM! ONE GIRL NAMED VENDY!

YOU KEEP HER OUT OF THE PICTURE, AND I'LL KEEP PETER PAN--
--TOO OCCUPIED TO BOTHER YOU AND YOUR PIRATES!
Hmmm... THAT SOUNDS LIKE A WIN-WIN SITUATION! YOU HAVE A DEAL!

NOK NOK
:yawn!: WHAT NOW, PETER? DO YOU KNOW WHAT TIME IT IS?!
2

SNOOK!
THAT'S CAPTAIN SNOOK TO YOU, MISSY! YOU'RE COMING WITH US!

LATER...
THIS IS ODD! VENDY SEEMS TO HAVE DISAPPEARED!
WHO KNOWS-- MAYBE SHE WISED UP AND JOINED THE CIRCUS!

LOOK! A FEATHER FROM CAPTAIN SNOOK'S HAT! HE MUST BE THE CULPRIT!
LET'S GO RESCUE HER!
ABOUT THAT... I HAVE A CONFESSION TO MAKE...

I ASKED CAPTAIN SNOOK TO KEEP HER OUT OF THE WAY SO THAT I COULD HAVE YOU ALL TO MYSELF!
BINKERBELL! YOU'RE A GREAT FRIEND-- BUT A RELATIONSHIP IS A BIT IMPRACTICAL!
LET'S DISCUSS IT AFTER RESCUING VENDY!
3

MEAN-WHILE...
OKAY, GIRL! JUST A FEW MORE STEPS! THAT CROCODILE IS HUNGRY AND HE MAY STOP CRAVING ME IF HE GETS A TASTE OF SOMEONE ELSE!
YOU FIEND!
THERE THEY ARE! WE HAVE TO SAVE HER!
I DIDN'T THINK THEY'D THREATEN HER LIFE!
LET'S GO!!
RELEASE VENDY, CAPTAIN SNOOK!!
AH, PETER PAN! WE MEET AGAIN!
HELP!
I-I'M LOSING MY BALANCE!
PIXIE DUST TO THE RESCUE!
SLURP!
SO MUCH FOR YOUR SUPPER, CROCODILE!
WE CAN FLY!
AND THAT DOES IT FOR YOU GUYS!
CURSES!
DARN IT!
4

OKAY GIRLS, LET'S SETTLE THIS THING ONCE AND FOR ALL!
BINK-- HAVE YOU MET MY LITTLE BROTHER?
LITTLE BROTHER?! I'M NO CRADLE ROBBER! IT'S YOU THAT I'M INTERESTED IN!
I KNOW I SAID LITTLE BROTHER, BUT HE'S REALLY MY TWIN!
TWEET
Oh, PAUL!
YES, PETER!
SEE! HE'S JUST LITTLE!
SO HE IS-- AND CUTER!
ZIP
WELL, I DON'T KNOW ABOUT THAT!
YOU SHOULD'VE INTRODUCED US SOONER!
HOLD ON A MINUTE! I THINK PAUL MAY BE THE CUTER ONE, TOO!
KEEP YOUR DISTANCE, YOU GANGLY GIANTESS!
Oh, BROTHER!
YOU SAID IT!
END

~~Betty & Veronica~~ Beau & Vernon in What if *Betty & Veronica* WERE GUYS?!

BEAU COOPER! WHAT BRINGS YOU HERE? I THOUGHT YOU WERE WORKING AT THE *GARAGE* TODAY!

WELL, IF IT ISN'T *VERNON LODGE*!

I *WAS* WORKING, BUT I TOOK OFF *EARLY* TO OFFICIALLY ASK *ARCHINA* TO THE *SCHOOL DANCE*!

POP'S MOM

BEAU

BILL GOLLIHER STORY

DAN PARENT PENCILS

BOB SMITH INKS

GLENN WHITMORE COLORS

JACK MORELLI LETTERS

HELLO, LADY AND FRIEND!
HAH HAH. VERY FUNNY, RICH BOY.

WHAT BRINGS THE BOTH OF YOU HERE TO MOM'S?
I WAS GOING TO ASK YOU TO THE DANCE LIKE WE TALKED ABOUT!
AND I TOLD HIM WE'VE ALREADY MADE PLANS!

OH, DEAR! I GUESS I DID GIVE YOU BOTH THE IDEA THAT I WOULD GO WITH YOU!
THAT COULD BE A PROBLEM!

WHY DON'T THE FOUR OF US JUST ALL GO TOGETHER?
I DON'T WANT A DATE!

NOT A DATE! JUST A GROUP OF FRIENDS ATTENDING A DANCE TOGETHER!
THAT SOUNDS FUN... NOT!

IF THAT'S WHAT ARCHINA WANTS TO DO, WE SHOULD RESPECT IT!
THANKS, BEAU! THEN IT WILL BE THE FOUR OF US!
AS LONG AS FOOD'S INVOLVED, I'LL BE THERE!
2

SEE YOU ALL SATURDAY!
PSST! VERNON!

LET ME GET THIS STRAIGHT... I JUST HEARD YOU AGREE TO A QUADRUPLE DATE WITH THOSE LOSERS? IT DOESN'T SEEM LIKE YOUR STYLE!
THAT'S RIGHT, REGINA!
BUT YOU KNOW I ALWAYS HAVE SOMETHING UP MY SLEEVE!

SATURDAY...
VERNON, THIS IS YOUR NEW SPORTS CAR!
YEAH-- DON'T YOU LOVE IT?

BUT WE WON'T HAVE ROOM TO PICK UP BEAU AND JUSTINE LIKE WE PLANNED!
OH, NO! YOU'RE RIGHT!
I FORGOT TO BRING THE LIMO, DIDN'T I?

AND SO...
I'M NOT BUYING THAT VERNON JUST FORGOT!
BUT I'LL BORROW MY DAD'S CAR AND PICK UP BEAU!
WE'LL MEET YOU GUYS AT THE DANCE!

BOOM
WHAT WAS THAT?!
OH, GREAT! IT FEELS LIKE WE'VE GOT A FLAT TIRE!
3

I'LL CALL THE MOTOR CLUB! NO NEED TO GET ALL MESSED UP BEFORE THE DANCE!
OKAY! JUSTINE'S CALLING!

WE'RE HERE! WHERE ARE YOU GUYS?
WE HAD A FLAT! VERNON CALLED THE MOTOR CLUB!

WHO KNOWS HOW LONG THAT WILL TAKE! YOU'LL MISS HALF THE DANCE! BUT IT CAN'T BE HELPED!
WHAT'S GOING ON?

LATER...
HEADLIGHTS! SOMEONE'S STOPPING!
MAYBE IT'S FINALLY THE MOTOR CLUB!

BEAU AND JUSTINE?! WHAT BRINGS YOU HERE? ARE YOU TRYING TO TAKE AWAY MY DATE?!
NO, SILLY! I'M HERE TO CHANGE YOUR TIRE SO YOU CAN GET TO THE DANCE!

ISN'T IT COMPLICATED ON THESE NEWER MODELS?
NAH! I DO IT ALL THE TIME DOWN AT THE GARAGE!
4

SOON!
WELL, WE MADE IT! THANKS TO BEAU!
I COULD'VE DONE IT MYSELF, BUT I DIDN'T WANT TO GET DIRTY!
NOW LET'S GET DANCING!
I PROMISED THE FIRST DANCE TO BEAU AFTER HE RESCUED US!
C'MON! I DON'T KNOW IF I'D CLASSIFY THAT AS A "RESCUE"!
WHEN DO I GET A CHANCE TO DANCE?
DON'T LOOK AT ME!
TWEET!
REGINA! WHAT A PLEASURE TO SEE YOU HERE!
I'M GOING TO LOSE MY APPETITE!
AND THAT'S SAYING SOMETHING!
Y'KNOW, I SHOULD JUST LET THOSE TWO GOODY-GOODIES BE! MAYBE WE'RE THE TWO WHO ARE MEANT FOR EACH OTHER!
I WAS WONDERING WHEN YOU WOULD SEE IT MY WAY!
HEY, YOU WITH THE FOOD TRAY-- COME HERE OFTEN?
END

Betty and Veronica
What if... Betty was really 'N AN ALIEN?!
ARCHIE! WE'VE FINALLY MANAGED TO GET SOME ALONE TIME...
HELLO, YOU TWO!
HOW DOES SHE DO THAT?!
BILL GOLLIHER STORY
DAN PARENT PENCILS
BOB SMITH INKS
GLENN WHITMORE COLORS
JACK MORELLI LETTERS
EVERY TIME I HAVE ARCHIE TO MYSELF, YOU MANAGE TO SHOW UP!
FLIP
AND WHY IS YOUR PONYTAIL DOING THAT?
DOING WHAT? Heh-Heh!
IT'S UP-- LIKE IT'S SCANNING THE SITUATION OR SOME-THING!
WEIRD!
1

FLIP
Oh! IT'S JUST... STATIC ELECTRI-CITY!
LOOKS LIKE YOU'RE NOT ALONE ANY-MORE...GUESS I'LL BE GOING!
I HAVE THINGS TO ATTEND TO!
AND SO...
THAT WAS CLOSE!
WHAT WERE YOU THINKING, PONIE?
SORRY... BUT THOSE TWO JUST GET ON MY NERVES!
WE CAN'T AFFORD TO LET ANYONE KNOW THAT I'M REALLY FROM ANOTHER WORLD... AND THAT YOU'RE MY FAITHFUL ALIEN MENTOR!
WHO HAS SERVED YOU WELL, AND INSTRUCTED YOU EVER SINCE WE WERE MAROONED ON THIS AWFUL PLANET!
WHILE YOU'VE WORKED TO REPAIR OUR SHIP ALL OF THESE YEARS!
THE REPAIRS ARE NOW FINALLY DONE! OUR TIME TO DEPART IS TONIGHT AT MIDNIGHT!
NOW LET'S GET BACK HOME QUICKLY SO I CAN MAKE OUR FINAL PREPAR-ATIONS!
OKAY, DO YOUR THING! START SPINNING!
BETTY?! WH-WHAT'S GOING ON?!
WHIRRRR
Oh... uh... HI, GUYS!
POP'S
NICE NIGHT FOR A PONY-TAIL FLIGHT!
2

SHALL I HYPNOTIZE THEM TO MAKE THEM FORGET?
NO, PONIE! I THINK IT'S TIME WE COME CLEAN--ESPECIALLY IF WE'RE LEAVING!
POP'S
I KNOW THIS WILL SOUND CRAZY, BUT I'M AN ALIEN, AND PONIE IS MY FAITHFUL COMPANION WHO POSES AS A HAIR EXTENTION!
uh... I THINK YOU'RE DOWNPLAYING ME A BIT!
AT LEAST THAT EXPLAINS WHY YOU'VE ALWAYS HAD THAT POOR FASHION PONY-TAIL!
DESTROY!
TAKE IT EASY, PONIE!
SO--IF YOU ARE AN ALIEN, WHY ARE YOU HERE?!
OUR SHIP WAS MAROONED HERE YEARS AGO--
--ON AN INFO GATHERING MISSION!
HE EVEN BUILT ROBOTIC PARENTS FOR ME SO I COULD PASS AS ONE OF YOU!
BUT NOW THE REPAIRS ARE DONE AND BETTY AND I SHALL BE LEAVING TONIGHT!
ARCHIE--COME WITH US! PLEASE! WE CAN SEE THE UNIVERSE TOGETHER!
BETTY, I CAN'T! THIS IS MY HOME!!
IT SURE IS!
3

Sniff! I UNDERSTAND!
PONIE, I'LL MEET YOU AT HOME IN TIME FOR THE FLIGHT! I JUST WANT TO BE ALONE FOR A WHILE!
BUT, BETTY...
HER SADNESS IS ALL THE FAULT OF YOU EARTHLINGS. FIRST, I'LL FREEZE YOU!!
BETTY! YOUR HAIR IS OUT OF CONTROL!
ZAP
URF!
NOW I'LL ATTACH MYSELF TO THIS ONE AND CONTROL HIS PUNY MIND!
WHAT BETTY WANTS, BETTY GETS!
POP
HEY, ARCH! WHERE ARE YOU GOING?
TO BETTY'S!
I HAVE BUSINESS TO ATTEND TO!

WHAT'S WITH THE CHEESY PONYTAIL?
WHO KNOWS--AND WHY WOULD HE BLEACH IT BLONDE?!

SOON...
VERONICA! WHAT ARE YOU DOING OUT HERE? SNAP OUT OF IT!
Huh?! WH-WHERE IS ARCHIE?
WE JUST PASSED HIM AND HIS BAD PONYTAIL EARLIER! HE WAS HEADED TO BETTY'S!
4

BAD PONYTAIL IS RIGHT! I'VE GOT TO STOP THEM BEFORE IT'S TOO LATE! WHAT TIME IS IT?!
MIDNIGHT ON THE DOT!
?

ZOOM
WOW! IT'S A UFO!
WE'RE TOO LATE! ARCHIE'S GONE FOREVER!

...AND THAT WAS THE CRAZY DREAM I HAD LAST NIGHT!
WOW! YOU'D BETTER BE MORE CAREFUL WHAT YOU EAT BEFORE GOING TO BED!
POOF
S

HELLO, EVERYONE! NOTICE ANYTHING DIFFERENT?
BETTY?!

Oh, NO!! IT'S TRUE!
HER PONYTAIL IS ON THE LOOSE!
FUNNY-- I THOUGHT I'D JUST TRY A SHORTER CUT!
I DIDN'T THINK IT WOULD CAUSE A STIR!
END

Betty and Veronica
in
THE BIG DILL!

BETTY! THERE'S A PICKLEBALL MIXED DOUBLES TOURNAMENT COMING UP AND I NEED YOU ON MY TEAM!
YOU'RE THE MOST OBSESSIVELY COMPETITIVE PERSON THAT I KNOW!
I'LL...TAKE THAT AS A COMPLIMENT!
KEEP OFF THE GRASS
TANIA DEL RIO STORY
JEFF SHULTZ PENCILS
JIM AMASH INKS
GLENN WHITMORE COLORS
JACK MORELLI LETTERS

LOOK! AND THE PRIZE IS THE BIGGEST DILL IN RIVERDALE! YOU KNOW HOW MUCH I LOVE PICKLES! I'VE JUST GOTTA WIN THIS!
BUT JUGHEAD... HAVE YOU EVER PLAYED PICKLEBALL BEFORE?

PSSH! HOW HARD CAN IT BE? IT'S BASICALLY OVERSIZED PING PONG!
OKAY, LET'S DO IT! I'LL RESEARCH SOME GAME STRATEGIES ONLINE AND SEND YOU SOME LINKS TO REVIEW.
WE'LL NEED TIME TO PRACTICE, OF COURSE!
SURE. WHATEVER.
1

THE NEXT DAY...
UGH, JUGHEAD! WHY AREN'T YOU ANSWERING?
EVERYTHING OKAY, BETTY?
JUGHEAD FLAKED ON ME! WE'RE SUPPOSED TO BE PRACTICING FOR THE BIG PICKLEBALL TOURNAMENT THIS WEEKEND!
JUGHEAD AND SPORTS? UNLESS IT'S COMPETITIVE EATING... ARE YOU REALLY SURPRISED?
I GUESS NOT!
BUT HEY, WHY DON'T YOU JOIN ME FOR SOME DRILLS? I'LL EVEN TEACH YOU A FEW THINGS!
IS THAT RIGHT?
SORRY, BETTY. THIS NEW DRESS IS MUCH TOO EXPENSIVE TO PERSPIRE IN!
BESIDES, I HAVE PLANS WITH MY DADDYKINS! SEE YOU LATER!
SIGH!
2

THE DAY OF THE BIG TOURNAMENT...
WOO HOO!
BOP
HOO-RAY!

≷yawn!≶ WHY DO THESE THINGS ALWAYS START SO EARLY?
THERE'S KEVIN AND TONI!
WE'RE YOUR FIRST ROUND OPPONENTS!

WOW! CHUCK AND NANCY ARE REALLY GOOD! THEY'RE THE ONES TO BEAT!

LOOK ALIVE, JUGHEAD! THAT BIG DILL IS MINE!
?
THOK

DINK
JUGHEAD! TONI'S SERVING! DID... YOU EVEN... BOTHER WATCHING... THE VIDEOS... I SENT?!
DONK
WOOSH
ZOOSH
SWOOF
POP
SWOOSH
3

PHEW! WE WON! JUST BARELY!
I KNEW YOU COULD DO IT!

I GUESS WE'LL BE FACING OFF AGAINST YOU TWO NEXT!
ACTUALLY, NO! WE JUST GOT DEFEATED BY THE REIGNING CHAMPS!

VERONICA?!
YOU PLAY PICKLEBALL?!
EVERY WEEKEND AT DADDY'S COUNTRY CLUB!

I'M KIND OF GLAD THAT I GOT ELIMINATED! RONNIE IS FIERCE ON THOSE COURTS!
NOT. HELPING.

SWOK
WAP
DONK

THE BACKHAND PICKLE PUNCH! I'VE READ ABOUT THAT TECHNIQUE!
WOOSH
4

SHORTLY...
WE LOST PRETTY BADLY. SORRY, JUGHEAD.
IT'S OKAY...

CONGRATS TO THE BIG DILLS OF RIVER-DALE!
TURNS OUT THE BIG DILL ISN'T EDIBLE, ANYWAY!

LUCKY FOR YOU, JUGGIE, THE CONSOLATION PRIZE IS A JAR OF CORNICHONS!
ALRIGHT!

CHEER UP, BETTY! COME BY THE CLUB SOMETIME AND I'LL TEACH YOU A FEW THINGS!

LIKE THAT BACKHAND PICKLE PUNCH?!
THAT... AND THE CENTERLINE BRINE!

OOH! HOW ABOUT THE DILLSPIN VOLLEY?
Mm-Hmm! BUT FIRST WE'LL NEED TO DO SOMETHING ABOUT YOUR OUTFIT! THE SECRET TO SUCCESS IS KNOWING THE GAME IS 90% MENTAL AND 10% FASHION!
LOOKS LIKE WE'RE ALL WINNERS!
END

Betty and Veronica in GETTING ANTSY!
DAN PARENT STORY & PENCILS
BOB SMITH INKS
GLENN WHITMORE COLORS
PICKENS PARK
JACK MORELLI LETTERS
?
!
1

?
!!

GASP!

SCAMPER SCAMPER

Ahhh!

FLIP
MUNCH MUNCH
?!
!!
ACK!
3

SCAMPER SCAMPER
SCAMPER
Ahhh!
FLOOP
MUNCH
MUNCH
MUNCH
?
!!
WINK
GRRR!
4

?!?
!
!
MARCH
MARCH
MARCH
HAHA!
FLING
ANTS!!
HA!
END

WHAT IF Betty & Veronica WERE MAD SCIENTISTS?

LATER...
THIS IS IT, RONNIE!
KRA-KOOM
THOSE JUMPERS ARE ADORABLE!
I KNOW, RIGHT?
WELCOME TO THE WORLD, LADIES! DO YOU KNOW WHAT TO DO?!
2

DESTROY!
DEMOLISH!
DELICIOUS!
OFF YOU GO!
HELP!
RARR!
GRR!
GRRARR!
RARRGH!
YIIIII!
3

ELSEWHERE...
WE REALLY DESERVE THIS!
YOU'RE SO RIGHT, RONNIE!
BY TOMORROW MORNING ALL OF RIVERDALE WILL BE LEVELED!
AND WE CAN START BUILDING RONNIE-DALE!
BETTYDALE!
MEANWHILE...
POP'S
POP'S
MINE!!
4

RRARRGH!!
POP'S
POP'S
POP'S
YAY!
THEY STOPPED EACH OTHER!!
HOORAY FOR ARCHIE!!
?!
AND YOU TWO ARE FINALLY GETTING THE VACATION YOU DESERVE!
The END

Betty and Veronica in RIVERDALE, LOVE IT OR LEAF IT!

Hi, Guys!

WHERE ARE YOU HEADED WITH ALL THE *GEAR?*

WE'RE CLEANING UP A PLETHORA OF *LEAVES* OVER AT MRS. HENDERSON'S!

BILL GOLLIHER • *STORY*
JEFF SHULTZ • *PENCILS*
JIM AMASH • *INKS*
GLENN WHITMORE • *COLORS*
JACK MORELLI • *LETTERS*

NO! I THINK I'LL START MY OWN ALL-GIRL LEAF CLEAN-UP TEAM!
IT COULD BE THE PERFECT GIMMICK TO MAKE SOME EXTRA CASH!

WE'LL CALL OURSELVES "THE LEAF LADIES"! NOW TO RECRUIT MY STAFF!
I DON'T NEED THE MONEY, BUT THE ENTERTAINMENT VALUE SHOULD BE ENOUGH FOR ME!

SO...
WELL, GIRLS, YOU KNOW THE MISSION, AND I ALREADY HAVE JOBS LINED UP! WHAT DO YOU SAY?
PUT TONI AND ETHEL DOWN AS A YES!
COUNT NANCY AND GINGER IN AS WELL!
MIDGE KLUMP IS ON THAT LIST, TOO! I COULDN'T ASK FOR A BETTER GROUP OF GIRLS TO GO INTO BUSINESS WITH!
Leaf LADIES

NEXT DAY...
ALRIGHT, LADIES! LET'S GET THOSE LEAVES MOVING!
SO! THE STORIES ARE TRUE! THE 'LEAF LADIES' ARE REAL!
Leaf LADIES
SCREECH

HEY! WHAT'S MOOSE DOING HERE? HE WAS HELPING WITH OUR GIGS!
DUH-- I KNOW, GUYS! BUT MIDGE IS A LEAF LADY! AND THIS WAY WE SPEND MORE TIME TOGETHER!
15
Leaf LADIES
2

TRAITOR!!
Oh, YEAH?! COME OVER HERE AND SAY THAT!!
NOW, NOW, MOOSE! THE LEAF LADIES ARE A PEACEFUL LOT!
ALL THE SAME, I THINK I'LL JUST STAY HERE!
AND SO...
WOW, ETHEL! I GUESS I SHOULD HAVE THOUGHT THIS THROUGH!
WHAT DO YOU MEAN, BETTY?

WHAT ARE WE NOW GOING TO DO WITH ALL THE LEAVES WE'VE COLLECTED? NO ONE WANTS US TO 'LEAF' THEM BEHIND!
DON'T WORRY, I'VE BEEN BUSY TAKING CARE OF THEM FROM ALL THE JOBS!
JUST KEEP 'EM COMING!

DAYS LATER...
Duh... ANOTHER DAY OF RAKING, AND ANOTHER TRUCKLOAD OF LEAVES!
YOU'RE A LIFE SAVER, MOOSE!

WHAT'S HE DOING WITH ALL THOSE?
WHO CARES? AS LONG AS HE GETS THEM OUT OF OUR WAY!
VROOM
3

NEXT MORNING...
Duh... COACH! WHAT ARE YOU DOING WITH THAT STORAGE ROOM?
I'M PLANNING TO CLEAN IT OUT TODAY! I'VE PUT IT OFF LONG ENOUGH!
STORAGE

ARE YOU SURE YOU WANT TO DO THAT, COACH?
OF COURSE, I'M SURE! I'M JUST GOING TO GET IN HERE AND...

KRASH
WHAT IN THE SAM HILL IS THIS?!

LEAVES?! WHERE DID THEY ALL COME FROM?!
Duh... TREES?
YUMPIN' YIMMINY!
VAT A MESS! I BETTER GO GET SOMETHING TO HELP CLEAN THIS UP!

I'LL GET MY STUFF OUT OF THE--
BROOM CLOSET
?

WHAM
OCK! I'VE BEEN LEAFED AS VELL!
MOOSE! WHAT'S GOING ON?!
4

IT'S NOT GOOD! THEY'RE FINDING ALL OUR LEAVES!
WHAT?!! YOU HID THEM HERE IN THE SCHOOL?!
IT SEEMED LIKE A GOOD IDEA!
I-IT DID?!
REALLY?!

MR. VEATHABEE! SOMEONE HAS BEEN STASHING BAGS OF LEAVES ALL OVER DA SCHOOL!
THAT'S RIDICULOUS!

I'M JUST GETTING IN-- BUT COME INTO MY OFFICE AND WE'LL DISCUSS IT!
GLADLY!
COACH

WOMP
WHAT IN THE WORLD--?!
EEK!!
COACH

OF ALL THE--! WHO'S GOING TO CLEAN UP ALL OF THESE LEAVES?!
Duh-- I'VE GOTTA RUN, BUT I KNOW SOME GIRLS WHO ARE GREAT AT THAT SORT OF THING!
END

Betty and Veronica in
TRICKY TREATS!
I'VE HAD IT WITH ALL OF THESE CURSED THINGS HAPPENING!
ME, TOO!
HOW ABOUT WE JUST PLAY IT LOW KEY AT MY HOUSE HANDING OUT CANDY TO TRICK-OR-TREATERS!
DAN PARENT STORY & PENCILS
BOB SMITH INKS
GLENN WHITMORE COLORS
JACK MORELLI LETTERS
SOUNDS LIKE A GOOD PLAN TO ME!
NOW THAT WE'VE GOTTEN RID OF THAT CURSED NECKLACE AND BRACELET, THINGS SHOULD BE FINE!
TRASH
1

SO...
JELLYBEAN! WE'RE SO GLAD YOU COULD JOIN US FOR HALLOWEEN!

THANKS, GIRLS! SHE WANTED TO SPEND TIME WITH HER FAVORITE BABYSITTERS!
WE'LL HAVE A GOOD TIME STAYING IN!

DING DONG
A TRICK-OR-TREATER IS HERE!

YOU CAN GIVE OUT THE CANDY, JELLYBEAN!
AREN'T YOU A CUTE LITTLE WITCH! YOU ALMOST LOOK LIKE YOU COULD FLY!

FLY!
WOOOSH
WHAT THE--?! H-HOW DID THAT HAPPEN?!
MOMMY! MOMMY!
2

COULD IT BE THE CURSE?!
OF COURSE NOT! THAT JEWELRY IS NOWHERE NEAR US ANYMORE!
DING DONG
LET'S TRY THIS AGAIN!
Ah! A DANCING PUMPKIN! HOW CUTE!
DANCING PUMPKINS?
Oh, MY GOSH!
ALL THE PUMPKINS ON THE STREET ARE DANCING!
THOSE LITTLE KIDS IN THE MONSTER COSTUMES ARE BEING CHASED BY THE PUMPKINS!
MONSTERS?
RARHR!
EEK!!
3

ARE THOSE REAL MONSTERS?!
THERE'S NO SUCH THING! BUT WE HAVE TO PROTECT JELLYBEAN!

EEK! ON HER WRIST!
IT'S THE CURSED BRACELET!!

HOW DID YOU GET THIS, JELLYBEAN?
JUGGIE!
OH, IT FIGURES THAT BUFFOON WOULD MESS THINGS UP!
VERONICA! WE NEED AN EXPERT TO RID US OF THESE CURSES ONCE AND FOR ALL!

AND THE EXPERT WE KNOW IS...

...Sabrina! THANKS FOR COMING!!
YOU SAID YOU HAD AN IDEA TO FIX THIS!
WE HOPE!
4

I DO! BUT FIRST... SOMETHING TO MAKE SURE THEY DON'T REMEMBER MY MAGIC!
I NEED TO SEND IT TO THE NETHER-WORLD... WHERE IT WILL BE UNABLE TO CAUSE HAVOC...
CURSED JEWELRY THAT I TOUCH... BE REMOVED FROM THIS WORLD AS SUCH...
BE CAST TO A PLACE WHERE NO HARM WILL BE... AND ONCE AND FOR ALL WE WILL BE FREE!!
THERE! IT'S GONE!
WHAT ABOUT THE OTHER PIECE... THE NECKLACE?
IF THERE'S ANOTHER PIECE OF JEWELRY, IT'S OUT OF MY RANGE...
LET'S HOPE IT'S SOMEWHERE WHERE IT CAN DO NO HARM!
AND...
WOW! WHO WOULD THROW AWAY A NICE NECKLACE LIKE THAT?! IT'LL MAKE A GREAT GIFT FOR MY AUNTIE!
TRASH
SO...
WHY MISS GRUNDY! WHAT A LOVELY NECKLACE!
ISN'T IT? MY NEPHEW GAVE IT TO ME!
THE END ...OR IS IT??

Betty and Veronica in Santa Baby!

I'M TIRED FROM ALL OF THIS HOLIDAY SHOPPING!
NOT ME! I'M JUST GETTING STARTED!

DAN PARENT STORY & PENCILS

BOB SMITH INKS | GLENN WHITMORE COLORS | JACK MORELLI LETTERS

WHY CAN'T I BE A NORMAL TEENAGER LIKE YOU TWO?
WELL, YOU ARE SANTA'S DAUGHTER! THAT'S NOT QUITE NORMAL!

BUT IT IS EXCITING!
NOT FOR ME! CAN I STAY WITH YOU GIRLS FOR AWHILE?

WELL, WE DO HAVE THIRTY SPARE BEDROOMS! I GUESS I CAN MAKE ROOM!
SO...

MS. NOELLE! WHAT WOULD YOU LIKE FOR BREAKFAST?
CAN I HAVE IT IN BED?

OF COURSE!

WHERE'S NOELLE?
SHE'S STILL IN BED!
Vague
2

WOW! SHE'S REALLY TAKING IT EASY!
I KNOW!
THAT'S MY JOB!

LATER!
ARE YOU GIRLS READY TO GO ICE SKATING?
I'M GOING TO STAY HERE AND HAVE A MANICURE AND A MASSAGE!
X-MAS TODAY

OKAY! SUIT YOURSELF! JOIN US IF YOU CAN!
I DON'T THINK SO-- I'LL BE WATCHING MOVIES IN THE SCREENING ROOM!

I THOUGHT SHE'D SPEND TIME WITH US! BUT YOUR HOUSE IS BASICALLY A SPA VACATION!

SO...
LET'S SEE WHAT I CAN WATCH...
HELLO, NOELLE!

DADDY! HOW DID YOU GET ON THIS SCREEN?!
I HAVE MY WAYS...
3

ARE YOU READY TO COME HOME YET?
NO! I'M ENJOYING THIS "ME TIME"!
I KNOW IT GETS OVERWHELMING BEING MY DAUGHTER, NOELLE!
I JUST NEED A BREAK FROM THE NORTH POLE! AND CHRISTMAS!
OKAY! WELL, YOU KNOW WHERE TO FIND ME!
'BYE, DADDY! I'LL BE RIGHT HERE DOING NOTHING!
LATER...
SHOULD WE ASK NOELLE TO JOIN US AT THE TOY DRIVE?
WHY BOTHER? SHE JUST WANTS TO STAY HOME AND KEEP PAMPERING HERSELF!
I WONDER WHAT THE GIRLS ARE UP TO!
Oh! IT'S ON FACESPACE LIVE!
IT'S THE TOY DRIVE AT THE HOSPITAL!
4

AWW... LOOK AT THE FACES ON THOSE KIDS!
ALL OF THIS PAMPERING HAS BEEN FINE...

BUT THIS IS WHAT CHRISTMAS IS ALL ABOUT!
I NEED TO GET DOWN THERE!

NOELLE! I'M SO GLAD YOU CAME DOWN!
ME, TOO!
DY DRIVE

SOMETIMES I FORGET THAT CHRISTMAS IS ABOUT GIVING!
WELL... RECEIVING IS PRETTY GREAT, TOO! BUT...

I GET WHERE YOU'RE COMING FROM!
I GUESS GIVING IS IN MY BLOOD!

I SHOULD PROBABLY GET BACK HOME! MY DAD MIGHT NEED ME!
THAT'S FOR SURE!
END

Betty and Veronica in LET'S HAVE A BALL!

BETTY! WHAT ON EARTH ARE YOU DOING?!

I'M MAKING THE WORLD'S LARGEST SNOWBALL!

DAN PARENT STORY & PENCILS

BOB SMITH INKS

GLENN WHITMORE COLORS

JACK MORELLI LETTERS

THE COMMITTEE IS COMING HERE THIS SATURDAY TO MEASURE IT!
DO YOU WANT TO HELP?
LOOK AT MY FACE! WHAT DOES IT TELL YOU?
I GUESS THAT'S A "PASS"!
YOU GOT IT!
BUT I'LL BE HERE SATURDAY FOR THE BIG EVENT!
WELL, THAT'S SWEET OF YOU!
BECAUSE IF THIS GETS ANY MEDIA COVERAGE--
--I MAY GET MY FACE ON NATIONAL TELEVISION!
AND THERE WE HAVE IT!
OKAY, ARCHIE-- BACK TO WORK! WE HAVE A WORLD'S RECORD TO BREAK!
2

A FEW DAYS LATER...
WOW! THAT'S BIG!!
IT'S A RECORD BREAKER!

BE HERE FOR THE BIG EVENT!
I WOULDN'T MISS IT!!

Phew! IT'S GETTING WARM! I HOPE THAT GIANT BALL DOESN'T MELT!

GULP!

SATURDAY ARRIVES...
IT'S BEEN WARM THESE PAST FEW DAYS!
HOW'S THE SNOW-BALL?

WE CAN AFFORD SOME MELTAGE, BUT NOT TOO MUCH!
3

I'LL CHECK IT WITH THIS TAPE MEASURE!

Oh, NO! WE'VE HAD SOME SHRINKAGE!
WE'VE DIPPED BELOW RECORD BREAKING SIZE!!

AND THE COMMITTEE IS HERE!!
ARCHIE! GATHER MORE SNOW FOR ME!

THERE'S NOT ENOUGH LEFT ON THE GROUND!
GO UP ON TURNER HILL BEHIND THE SCHOOL! AND BRING THE WHEEL-BARROW!

VERONICA! HELP HIM-- PLEASE!!
Oh, OKAY! BUT I WANT CREDIT FOR THIS IN THE MEDIA COVERAGE!

SO...
OKAY, RON! I THINK WE HAVE ENOUGH SNOW NOW!
THEN LET'S GO!
4

UGH! THIS IS HEAVY!!
I COULD USE SOME HELP!
THAT'S NOT MY STYLE!
CAN'T-- KEEP IT-- STEADY--
UGH! UMPH! URK!!
BOOF
URK!
WE'RE GATHERING SPEED--AND SNOW!
LOOK OUT BELOW!!
KRASH
LOOKS LIKE I'M NOT GOING TO BREAK THE RECORD FOR BIGGEST SNOWBALL...
NO... BUT YOU HAVE BROKEN THE RECORD FOR THE BIGGEST HUMAN SNOWBALL!
WELL, RON...
...YOU WANTED YOUR MOMENT IN THE SPOT-LIGHT!
END

ARCHIE 80TH ANNIVERSARY

KENNEDY BROS.—BOB SMITH

Archie in CRISIS ON THE RIVERDALE EARTHS

NO! I'M THE TIME POLICE, AND I NEED HELP FROM YOU...

...YOUR EARTH'S ARCHIE ANDREWS!

YOU'RE SAYING THERE'S MORE THAN ONE OF ME, TOO?!

DON'T LET WEATHERBEE HEAR ABOUT THIS!

ANDREWS

4VIC

BILL GOLLIHER WRITER

THE FAB K-BROS! PENCILS

BOB SMITH INKS

JACK MORELLI LETTERS

GLENN WHITMORE COLORS

1

OF COURSE, THERE'S...
ARCHIE ONE...
ARCHIE 3000...

HOLLYWOOD ARCHIE...
WHY SO SERIOUS?

LITTLE ARCHIE...
NEW LITTLE ARCHIE...
NOT TO BE CONFUSED WITH THE NEW ARCHIES...
...AND EVEN ARCHIE BABIES!

MY PLAIN OL' ARCHIE HEAD IS SPINNING!
I'M SURE, BUT WE'VE GOT A UNIVERSE TO SAVE, OLD FRIEND!

THEY MAROONED ME ON THIS WORLD TO KEEP ME OUT OF THE WAY OF THEIR PLANS!
WHO?! WHAT PLANS?!
2

I'M SORRY! IT SEEMS MAD DOCTOR DOOM--LITTLE ARCHIE'S NEMESIS--HAS CROSSED DIMENSIONS!
WHERE HE JOINED UP WITH EVILHEART--PUREHEART'S NEMESIS--TO HATCH A PLAN TO COLLAPSE ALL OF THE CONTINUUMS INTO ONE!

SO? WHAT'S THAT GOT TO DO WITH ME??
I'M STUCK HERE UNLESS I'M ABLE TO GET YOUR HELP TO DEFEAT THEM!

HOW?!
MY TIME TRAVEL BEANIE HAS BEEN MODIFIED FOR THE CURRENT CRISIS NOT ONLY TO TRAVEL THROUGH TIME, BUT INTO OTHER ARCHIE DIMENSIONS!

I ALSO HAVE THE ABILITY TO TRANSFORM YOU INTO ANY VERSION OF ARCHIE FROM THE OTHER REALITIES!
LIKE I JUST DID!
OKAY! SOUNDS MORE INTERESTING THAN WHAT I HAD PLANNED FOR THIS EVENING!

FIRST, I'LL HAVE YOU BECOME PUREHEART THE POWERFUL--ONE OF THE SUPER TEENS!
COOL! I FEEL LIKE ONE OF THOSE CONVENTION COSPLAY GUYS!
KLIK
KZZNG
3

LET'S GO! NEXT STOP--THE DIMENSIONAL GATEWAY!
KLIK

WELL! LOOK WHO'S HERE AT THE DIMENSIONAL GATEWAY THAT WE'RE COLLAPSING!
POOPHEAD THE POWERLESS AND THE TIME COP!
BZZT
KZZZZNNG

NOW YOU'RE BOTH OUT OF TIME AND AT OUR COMBINED MERCY!
NOT SO FAST! WE'VE GOT A PLAN!

I'M SENDING YOU BOTH BACK TO YOUR YESTERDAYS! THE POINT BEFORE YOU COMBINED FORCES!
THIS WAY WE CAN TAKE THEM ON INDIVIDUALLY!
BRZORP

SOON...
HEY! WHAT'S HAPPENING TO ME??!
I'M TRANSFORMING YOU INTO A LITTLE ARCHIE VERSION OF PUREHEART SO YOU CAN TAKE ON MAD DOCTOR DOOM IN RIVERDALE!
COOL BEANS!
KZZZZ ZZNNG
MAD DOCTOR DOOM'S LAB
4

NICE PAJAMAS, LITTLE ARCHIE!
THANKS FOR THE COMPLIMENT! BUT I'M STILL ABOUT TO KNOCK YOUR SOCKS OFF!
KRASH
OOF!
HOW CAN A KID HAVE THAT MUCH POWER?!
HE'S NOT JUST A KID, HE'S LITTLE PUREHEART!
BOOMP

MAYBE SO, BUT HE'LL BE NO MATCH FOR MY LATEST TOOL!
I HAVE DISCOVERED THERE ARE MULTIPLE VERSIONS OF RIVERDALE OUT THERE AND I AM REACHING OUT TO A FELLOW VILLIAN IN ANOTHER!

TOGETHER WE CAN COMBINE FORCES AND COLLAPSE ALL OF THE REALITIES INTO ONE FOR THE TWO OF US TO RULE!
DON'T COUNT YOUR WORLDS DOMINATION PLANS BEFORE THEY HATCH, BUBBY!
SOK

HURRY, ARCHIE! HE'S GETTING IN TOUCH WITH EVILHEART!
YEAH? WHO'S THERE?!
DON'T WORRY--I'M ON IT! I'LL USE HIS OWN EQUIPMENT TO BUILD HIM A MAKESHIFT PRISON!
JEEPERS! WHAT'S GOING ON HERE?!
5

THAT SHOULD TAKE CARE OF MAD DOCTOR DOOM!
GIRLS, KEEP AN EYE ON HIM UNTIL WE GET BACK!
SURE THING, BIG JUGHEAD AND SUPER LITTLE ARCHIE!
DON'T FORGET, YOU STILL HAVE ANOTHER VILLAIN TO BEAT, ARCHIE ANDREWS!

DOOM IS RIGHT! EVILHEART IS FROM THE SAME CONTINUUM AS PUREHEART! WON'T WE BE PRETTY EQUAL POWER-WISE?
EXACTLY! WE HAVE TO TRY SOMETHING ALL-NEW TO WIN!

VOILA!
ARCHIE PUREHEART 3000!
KLIK
WOW! I SEE THAT MULLETS MAKE A COMEBACK IN THE FUTURE!
KZZZNNNG
6

AND SO...
EVILHEART! IT SEEMS I'M HERE TO PUT YOU IN YOUR PLACE ONCE AGAIN!
WELL, WELL! CUTE NEW OUTFIT, PUREHEART! BUT YOU'RE STILL THE SAME GOODY-GOODY LOSER!
RIGHT, GIRLS?!
EEK!
POP'S

I THINK YOU'LL FIND THIS BATTLE A LITTLE LESS OF A MATCH-UP FOR YOU!
WE'LL SEE ABOUT THAT, LONG HAIR!
WHAM

I'M OVER HERE, BAD BOY! THAT WAS JUST A HOLOGRAM!
YOU'LL ONLY GET AWAY WITH THAT ONCE!
KA-BAM

ON SECOND THOUGHT, MAYBE TWICE!
YOU SEE, I'M COMBINED WITH ARCHIE 3000, SO MY FUTURE TECH CAN KICK YOUR 20th CENTURY PATOOTIE!

YOU'RE TALKING GIBBERISH, PUREHEART! NOW YOU'RE DONE FORROOOW!
ONE 31ST CENTURY PARALYZING RAY COMING UP!
BZZT
7

IT APPEARS HE'S GONE FROM EVILHEART TO FROZENHEART!
GRAB HIM! WE'LL HOOK BACK TO LITTLE ARCHIE RIVERDALE FOR MAD DOCTOR DOOM!

SOON...
HOW DO YOU PROPOSE WE KEEP THESE TWO FROM MAKING FURTHER TROUBLE?
Hmmm! I'VE GOT IT!

NEXT STOP, ANOTHER OF THE ENDLESS ARCHIE DIMENSIONS!
A WORLD THAT WILL DEFINITELY KEEP THEM IN THEIR PLACE!

WELCOME TO YOUR NEW HOME, BOYS! THE ZOMBIE WORLD OF AFTERLIFE WITH ARCHIE!
ZOMBIES?! THEY WON'T APPRECIATE MY BRAIN--THEY'LL EAT IT!

YOU COULD CONSIDER THAT BEING APPRECIATED! RIGHT, ZOMBIE JUGHEAD?
GRRR!!

WAIT! YOU CAN'T LEAVE US HERE! I HAVE AN EXCEPTIONALLY LARGE BRAIN!
SO DO I!
I THINK!
YUM!!
TA-TA! BETTER GET A HEAD START!
8

THAT NOISE! IT SOUNDS LIKE A STAMPEDE! THE GROUP IS COMING INTO VIEW!
NO! IT CAN'T BE!
IT'S HUNDREDS OF BETTYS AND VERONICAS--EACH FROM A RESCUED DIMENSION--WHO WANT TO THANK YOU!

MAKE A PROPER LINE, GIRLS! YOU'LL EACH GET YOUR CHANCE!
SMOOCH SMOOCH SMOOCH
SMOOCH
SMOOCH
THIS IS NICE, BUT IT'S TOO MUCH!
I CAN'T BREATHE!

SLURRPP
SLURP
SLURP
VEGAS?! IT'S JUST YOU?! WHAT A DREAM!

I GUESS IT JUST GOES TO SHOW YOU ALL THE ENDLESS POSSIBILITIES ONE LIFE CAN HOLD IN THE UNIVERSE!
OR WAS IT??

BUT JUST TO BE SAFE...
...IT'S THE LAST TIME I EVER GET TAKE OUT FROM THAT DUMP!
Jughead's DINER Est. 1990
SAT NITE BINGO!
The END

Archie in HAPPY Archieversary!

THERE IT IS! THE *FIRST-EVER* ISSUE OF *"ARCHIE"*! I CAN'T BELIEVE IT'S BEEN *EIGHTY YEARS* SINCE I FIRST SHOWED UP IN A COMIC BOOK!

ANGELO DeCESARE STORY

The FAB K-BROS! PENCILS

JIM AMASH INKS

GLENN WHITMORE COLORS

JACK MORELLI LETTERS

YOU'D BETTER THINK AGAIN, PAL!
YEAH! IT SOUNDS TO ME LIKE A ONE-PERSON OPINION POLL!
?!

I'M THE FELLOW WHO MADE ARCHIE POPULAR IN THE FIRST PLACE!
AND I'M THE DUDE WHO'S KEPT US POPULAR ALL AROUND THE WORLD!
POP

HEY, I HAVE A TON OF RESPECT FOR WHAT YOU GUYS HAVE DONE...

...BUT SINCE I'M THE NEWEST ARCHIE, IT STANDS TO REASON THAT I'M THE MOST PERFECT ARCHIE!

DING DING
HOLD ON, GUYS! THE ALARM ON MY PHONE JUST WENT OFF!
THAT'S A PHONE?!

OH, NO! MY PARENTS AND ALL MY FRIENDS ARE THROWING ME AN EIGHTIETH ANNIVERSARY PARTY AND IT TOTALLY SLIPPED MY MIND!
2

WHAT A TIME FOR MY CAR TO BE IN THE REPAIR SHOP... AGAIN!
IF I START RUNNING NOW MAYBE I CAN GET HOME BEFORE THE PARTY'S OVER!
WAIT UP, YO! IT'S OUR ANNIVERSARY TOO!
AND MY CAR IS RIGHT OUTSIDE!
PEP

THERE IT IS!
I SEE IT-- BUT WHAT IS IT?!
AND WHO ARE THOSE SPACE ALIENS?
WHAT TOOK YOU SO LONG, ARCHIE?
I DIDN'T MIND WAITING FOR YOU!
MUNCH!
I DID! I'M STARV-ING!

PILE IN, FELLAS! I'LL GET US HOME!
SAY... HE'S A DREAM-BOAT!
SO IS HE!
SOME THINGS NEVER CHANGE!
MUNCH!

HERE WE GO! HOT DIGGITY-DOG!
DUDE, WHERE ARE THE SEAT BELTS?!
HONK
Z
3

I DON'T GET IT! I JUST PATCHED THOSE TIRES TODAY!
MAN, FORGET THIS RELIC! I'VE GOT A REAL CAR RIGHT ACROSS THE STREET!
POW
POW
HSSS

THERE'S ARCHIE!
BUT WHO'S THAT WITH HIM?
AM I THE ONLY ONE FREAKING OUT HERE?!
WE CAN HANG LATER, PEOPLE! RIGHT NOW I'VE GOT SOMETHING TO PROVE!

SOON...
SKREE
HERE WE ARE!

I TOLD YOU I'D GET US HOME! I GUESS THIS PROVES WHO THE COOLEST ARCHIE IS!
R
4

WHOA!
THUMP
KRASH
WHAT'S GOING ON HERE?!
MOM! DAD! I'M SORRY I'M LATE FOR MY BIG EIGHTIETH ANNIVERSARY PARTY!
THAT'S NOT UNTIL TOMORROW, ARCHIE!
I GUESS YOU MADE A MISTAKE!
I MAKE A LOT OF MISTAKES, DAD, BUT I KEEP TRYING!
WHAT ELSE IS NEW? I'VE BEEN TRYING FOR EIGHTY YEARS!
TRYING TO DO THE RIGHT THING! THAT'S WHAT'S IMPORTANT!
WHAT'S IMPORTANT IS THAT NO MATTER WHAT YEAR OR WHAT DECADE IT IS, ARCHIE IS ALWAYS ARCHIE!
THAT'S WHY WE LOVE YOU, SON!
AND WHY THE WHOLE WORLD LOVES YOU... AND ALWAYS WILL!
for VICTOR!
END

Archie
IN
HAPPY MANY-VERSARY!
HAPPY ANNIVERSARY, ARCHIE!
WHAT'S THE OCCASION?
UH, THANKS, BETTY!
CRAIG BOLDMAN : STORY
BILL GOLLIHER PENCILS
JIM AMASH INKS
GLENN WHITMORE COLORS
JACK MORELLI LETTERS
IT WAS ONE YEAR AGO TODAY THAT ARCHIE BAKED ME A FROZEN PIZZA!
HUH?!
OH, YEAH... I GUESS I REMEMBER THAT!
BETTY HAD PLAYED IN A TOURNAMENT WITH HER BALL TEAM...
1

"IT WAS A LONG DAY AND SHE DIDN'T FEEL LIKE GOING OUT, SO I JUST POPPED A PIZZA IN THE OVEN..."
THAT'S IT?!
BETTY'S ALWAYS BEEN LIKE THAT! SHE COMMEMORATES LITTLE EVENTS!
I ENJOY A FROZEN PIZZA--BUT IT HARDLY QUALIFIES AS AN "EVENT"!
I AGREE! BUT SHE'S FUNNY THAT WAY!
THE NEXT DAY!
ANOTHER ANNIVERSARY?
EIGHTEEN MONTHS AGO TODAY!
WE RAKED LEAVES TOGETHER!
AH! GOOD MEMORY, BETTY!
ARCH, YOU'RE KIDDING!
SHE'S A LITTLE QUIRKY, I ADMIT, BUT WHAT DOES IT HURT? IT'S SWEET!
2

AND!
DON'T TELL ME!
IT WAS A SHORT SIX WEEKS AGO! HAPPY ANNI-VERSARY!
POP'S
ANNIVERSARY OF WHAT, MAY I ASK?
OF THAT TIME YOU BUMPED YOUR HEAD!
WHICH TIME?!
AND BUMPED IT ON WHAT?
HE BUMPED IT ON MY HEAD!
Ah!
SUDDENLY IT ALL STARTS MAKING SENSE!
I DON'T KNOW WHY YOU KEEP TRACK OF SUCH EVENTS, BUT HAPPY ANNIVERSARY TO YOU, TOO!
OKAY, BETTY, I'VE WATCHED THE OTHERS BEING BAFFLED BY YOUR BEHAVIOR, BUT I KNOW THERE'S GOT TO BE MORE TO THESE STORIES!
POP'S
REALLY? SUCH AS?
WHY WOULD YOU FEEL MOVED TO COMMEMORATE A FROZEN PIZZA?!
Oh! THE PIZZA.
3

"MY TEAM HAD LOST BADLY. I NEEDED CHEERING UP."
"I WAS ACHY AND TIRED AND ASKED ARCHIE TO PUT A PIZZA IN THE OVEN...
"AND WHEN IT CAME OUT..."
YOU'RE ALWAYS A WINNER IN MY BOOK, BETTY!
OKAY, THAT WAS SWEET. BUT WHAT ABOUT RAKING LEAVES?
WELL...
"MRS. WOODIWISS DEPENDED ON HER SON TO DO THE YARDWORK AROUND HER HOUSE."
HEY, MRS. W! WHAT'S HAPPENED, BRAD?
I'VE SPRAINED MY ANKLE AND CAN'T RAKE!
"ARCHIE NEVER SAID A WORD--HE JUST GOT TO WORK!"
4

Hmm. AND THE BUMPED HEAD?
ARCHIE REMEMBERED THAT THE WIGGINS' DOG HAD BEEN MISSING!
MISSING
DOG
HEY, THAT'S POOCHINI! THE POOR PUP IS UPSET AND JITTERY! I'LL CIRCLE AROUND THIS WAY, AND YOU COME UP FROM BEHIND!
"THE DOG WAS SLIPPERY!
BONK
"BUT IN THE END, WE GOT HIM HOME FOR A HAPPY REUNION!"
BUT BETTY-- ARCHIE DOESN'T REMEMBER THOSE DETAILS!
NATURALLY NOT! HE DIDN'T DO ALL THOSE THINGS TO SHOW OFF OR EARN CREDIT!
HE JUST DOES THEM BECAUSE HE'S ARCHIE!
FOR HIM, THOSE ARE ORDINARY DAYS!
BUT FOR ME, THEY ARE DAYS I'LL NEVER FORGET!
The END

Archie in
POUR SOME SUGAR ON ME
SHOULD THE BAND REHEARSE TODAY?
WHY? WE DON'T HAVE ANY GIGS COMING UP!
DAN PARENT STORY & PENCILS
BOB SMITH INKS
GLENN WHITMORE COLORS
JACK MORELLI LETTERS
WHAT?! THAT'S UNUSUAL! WE SHOULD HAVE SOMETHING LINED UP!
WELL, IT'S BEEN SLOW LATELY!
MAYBE WE SHOULD SHAKE THINGS UP!
HOW SO?
1

WE COULD TRY EXPERIMENTING WITH OUR SOUND!
LOOK AT THIS POSTER!

A CONCERT FOR THE DECADES FESTIVAL!
The DECADES
THE GROOVY GUYS
The B-6's
RUSTY McGEE
THE ZITZ
LED AIRPLANE
THE ROLLING ROCKS
THESE ARE BANDS OUR PARENTS LIKED!

AND GRAND-PARENTS!
the DECAD
THE GROOVY GUYS
RUSTY McGEE
LED AIRPLA

WELL, I LOVE ELIZA FITZGERALD!
SHE WAS A TORCH SINGER IN THE 1950s!

I CAN JUST SEE MYSELF BELTING OUT THOSE TORCH SONGS IN MY GLAMOROUS GOWNS...

UH... ONE THING, RON--
--WE'RE A BAND! WHAT ABOUT THE REST OF US?!
2

OH, WELL! YOU CAN BE MY BACK-UP BAND!
NEXT IDEA!
The BEATS! NOW THEY HAD A CLASSIC 1960s SOUND!
THEY WERE PRETTY AWESOME!
The BEATS

THEY WERE ALL GUYS, THOUGH!
WE HAVE GUYS AND GIRLS IN OUR BAND!

THAT'S WHERE A 1970s PUNK BAND LIKE "The SLASHES" COMES IN!

PUNK ROCK WAS OPEN TO EVERYBODY! GUYS! GIRLS! YOU DIDN'T EVEN HAVE TO KNOW HOW TO PLAY YOUR INSTRUMENTS!
THAT'S GOOD FOR ARCHIE THEN!
3

I THINK WE SHOULD CONSIDER ONE OF US GIRLS AS THE LEAD SINGER -- LIKE THAT GIRL BAND FROM THE 1980s... The GA-GAs!!
WELL... I THINK PEOPLE ARE USED TO ME ON LEAD VOCALS!
BUT I SUPPOSE YOU COULD SING A SONG OR TWO!
OH, GEE, THANKS! WE'LL DISCUSS THIS FURTHER!
I THINK WE NEED A HARDER SOUND!
TAKE THE 1990s WHEN THE GRUNGE SCENE CAME IN! PEARL JELLY WAS ALL THE RAGE!
AS WAS NERVE TRAUMA!
WELL, WE CAN TRY THAT!
4

THE NEXT DAY AT REHEARSAL...
SUGAR SUGAR
The Archies

I DON'T KNOW! SLOW IT DOWN A BIT!
AND ADD A BASS LINE!

AND A LITTLE MORE KEYBOARD!
SUGAR SUGAR
THAT'S PERFECT! WONDERFUL!!
HONEY HONEY

YEAH! IT SOUNDS PERFECT ALL RIGHT!
EXCEPT FOR ONE THING--

--THAT'S EXACTLY HOW WE USUALLY PLAY IT!
WELL, I GUESS YOU CAN'T MESS WITH PERFECTION!
end

Archie in PEP TO THE FUTURE!

NEWSPAPER ROOM
MAGAZINES & PERIODICALS
IS MISS GRUNDY'S ASSIGNMENT ON THE *HISTORY OF RIVERDALE* MAKING YOU FALL OVER IN *BOREDOM*, ARCHIE?
NOW I KNOW WHY SHE ALWAYS TELLS ME NOT TO LEAN BACK IN MY CHAIR, JUGHEAD!

FRANCIS BONNET STORY
THE FAB K-BROS! PENCILS
JIM AMASH INKS
GLENN WHITMORE COLORS
JACK MORELLI LETTERS

WHOA!
THIS LOOKS LIKE THE 1940s!
AND THAT GUY LOOKS LIKE YOU!
MLJ MOVERS
JUST A MATTER OF SKILL, THAT'S ALL!

AND TA' THINK FOR MY NEXT TRICK I WAS GONNA BE BLIND-FOLDED!
KRAK

HYAH. M'NAME'S ARCHIE, BUT CALL ME CHICK. YOU'RE NEW HERE, AIN'T YOU?
MOVING IN TODAY! I'M BETTY COOPER AND YOU ALMOST CRASHED INTO ME!

WHAT A WAY TO NOT START A FRIENDSHIP!
THIS BIKE DOESN'T FIT THE TIME PERIOD!
AND NEITHER DO WE!

WE'RE IN SOME SORT OF ALTERNATE UNIVERSE RIVERDALE FROM 1941, AND THAT SCENE WAS SUPPOSED TO PLAY OUT DIFFERENTLY!
GULP! IS THAT BAD?!
2

WE CAUSED A RIFT IN TIME AND SPACE! IF WE DON'T GET THINGS BACK ON TRACK, IT COULD DESTROY THE UNIVERSE!
THAT DEFINITELY SOUNDS BAD!

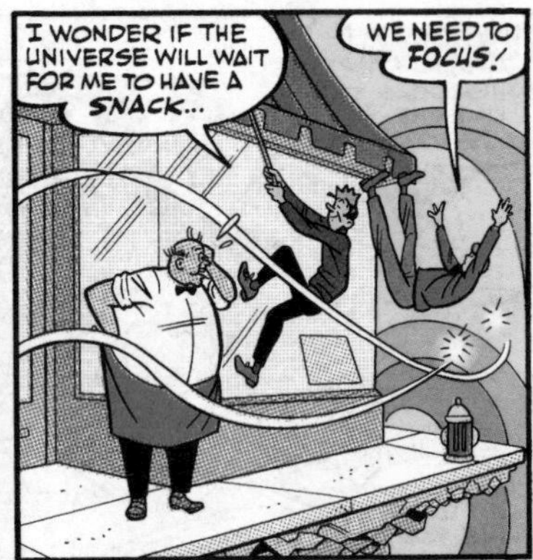
I WONDER IF THE UNIVERSE WILL WAIT FOR ME TO HAVE A SNACK...
WE NEED TO FOCUS!

ACCORDING TO THIS BOOK, ALTERNATE YOU IS SUPPOSED TO RUIN OLD MAN COOPER'S PAINTING!
I WONDER IF THAT'S SOMETHING I COULD DO...

I NEVER DOUBT YOUR ABILITY TO MAKE A MESS OF THINGS!
SHRIPP

MY PORTRAIT! RUINED! YOU IMBECILE!
THIS GUY SURE SOUNDS A LOT LIKE MR. LODGE!
3

SORRY, SIR! I CAN MAKE IT UP TO YOU BY HELPING AT YOUR CARNIVAL NEXT WEEK!
I THINK THAT'S A GREAT IDEA, DADDY! HE'S SO FUNNY!
FINE! YOU CAN WALK THE TIGHT-ROPE!

BETTY HAS A CRUSH ON YOU IN ANY UNIVERSE!
HEY, YOU TWO LOOK-A-LIKES! I DON'T KNOW WHERE YOU CAME FROM, BUT I'M GONNA SEND YOU BACK!

I HOPE THE UNIVERSE DOESN'T FALL APART IN THE MEANTIME!

GULP! I WISH THAT THERE WAS AN EASIER WAY TO SAVE THE UNIVERSE!
TAFFY

Y-YIII!
BOO! YOU AIN'T AS GOOD ON A TIGHTROPE AS ME!
IT'S A SHAME TO WASTE THESE DELICIOUS TOMATOES ON HIM!

EEP!
I KNOW I'M SUPPOSED TO FALL -- BUT NOT THIS EARLY!
SPLAT
4

DON'T WORRY, ARCHIE! I'VE GOT YOU!
THANKS, JUGHEAD!
THOSE TWO STOLE OUR NAMES, TOO?!
IMITATION IS THE SINCEREST FORM OF FLATTERY!

GLUB! GLUB! JUSH WAIT'LL I GET MY HANDS ON BOTH THOSE CLUMSY KIDS!

POOF
WE'RE BACK!
WE MUST HAVE SUCCESSFULLY SAVED THE UNIVERSE-- AND THE SPACE-TIME CONTINUUM!
PICKLES

LET'S PUT THIS BOOK BACK WHERE WE FOUND IT!
WE DEFINITELY WOULDN'T WANT SOMETHING LIKE THIS TO HAPPEN AGAIN!
PICKLES

NOPE! AT LEAST NOT FOR ANOTHER 80 YEARS!
END